Two Different Worlds

"I'm going to ask you something," said Kathy. The look in her eyes worried me. She was so angry. "Is modeling suddenly more important than us?"

"Of course not!" I blurted out desperately. It was true. I was simply doing the best I could to juggle two different worlds.

"Then how could you forget about this dance? We've been planning it and talking about going for weeks," she went on.

"I know," I said. "But there was no way I could have predicted everything that happened."

"Don't bother coming over tonight," Kathy grumbled. "Why should you help if you're not going to the dance, anyway?"

"But I want to help," I insisted.

"No you don't," she said as she started to walk away from me. "You want to be a famous model."

Cover
Kids

Nicole's Chance

Suzanne Weyn

Troll Associates

Published by Troll Associates.

Nicole's Chance

Chapter One

I can't do this," I said, stopping short as we turned by the corner of Maple's department store at the Appleton Mall. In front of me was a swelling, surging sea of girls. "This is definitely not a good idea," I told my friend Dee Forrest.

Dee looked back up at me with excited, shining eyes. "Nikki Wilton, you are the prettiest eighth-grade girl in all of Thomas Dewey Junior High School. If you can't win this modeling contest, nobody can."

"But look how many girls are trying out!" I wailed, feeling icy fingers of panic running up my spine.

My other good friend, Kathy Dillon, grabbed hold of my wrist and pulled me toward the crowd. "You can't chicken out now. We've spent the last week talking you into this. There's no sense discussing it anymore. You have to do this, Nikki."

"No I don't," I protested as I pulled away.

"Yes you do," Kathy said firmly. "You already look like a model, so you might as well be one."

"Yeah, Kathy's right." Dee laughed, tossing back her long, dark curls. "You have the height and that beautiful red hair. We're counting on you to get rich and invite us to fabulous parties where we can meet celebrities."

Kathy brushed her blond bangs from her forehead and then pulled me along, trying to blaze a trail through the crowd. "You owe it to us, Nikki," she said with a teasing smile. "Aren't we your closest, dearest, most wonderful friends?"

"Yes, but…" I stammered.

"But nothing! We want to know someone who is rich and famous," Kathy went on. "You're our only hope."

"Okay, okay." I gave in, laughing despite my nervousness. Ever since the day Dee saw the flier announcing this model search contest, she had hounded me to try out. Kathy and a couple of other friends jumped into it one day while we were eating together in the cafeteria, and soon I had no choice but to agree to go for it. My friends were positive I could win the contest. I wished I shared their confidence.

The Calico Modeling Agency was looking for five "fresh, lovely young faces." That's what the pink fliers they'd dropped off at school had said, anyway.

If it hadn't been for my friends insisting, I'd never have come down here to try out. For one thing, when I looked in the mirror, I didn't see a model. Okay, my hair is an unusual auburn, but it's dead straight. I would have much preferred a ton of curls like some redheads have.

I have large eyes, but my lashes are blond at the tips so they look short, and I have freckles across my cheeks, which I loathe and despise. Thank goodness my mouthful of metal braces came off last month. I have to admit, my teeth do finally look straight. Still, unless they needed models for toothpaste ads, I didn't think that would be enough to make me a model.

Kathy was doing a good job of wiggling her way through the crowd toward the registration table. She held my wrist tightly, while Dee kept one hand on my back.

Suddenly a female voice boomed over a loudspeaker. "Please make five separate lines. Begin each line behind a colored pennant." Looking up, I saw triangular pennants hanging on a wire strung above the table. The first flag was yellow.

All around me, girls scrambled to get a good place in the lines that were forming. "Come on," said Kathy. "Stay with me behind this yellow one. Maybe we'll get up there faster and won't have to wait long."

"You have to promise me one thing, Nikki," Dee said as we followed Kathy through the crowd.

"What?"

"If you ever get to ride in a limousine, you'll come by and pick me up. I've always wanted to ride in one."

"I promise," I said. "Only you might have to wait for

our junior prom for that."

"No way, that's years off," Dee protested. "I want my limousine ride in about six months. I figure that's how long it should take for you to hit the limo stage. And I hope it has a car phone so I can call everyone I know. Think of that! I could spend hours on the phone without my parents telling me to cut it short."

"I'll do my best," I said doubtfully. "But don't be too disappointed if I don't make it."

As I stood fighting down my nervousness, I noticed that the girl behind Dee was hiccuping like crazy. She was slightly plump, with blond, frizzy curls. Standing beside her was another girl with very dark brown hair who was wearing a faded black turtleneck, scruffy jeans, and dark sunglasses.

"Doris, just calm down, would ya?" I heard the dark-haired girl grumble to her friend. "This is a dumb idea, anyway. Let's get out of here."

Doris clutched the other girl's arm. "You can't leave me now, Tracey," she said desperately. Then she hiccuped two times. "This is my chance, my big chance to be a model. Puh-lease, don't go. You know how important this is to me. I'll die if they don't pick me."

"Oh, you won't die," Tracey scoffed.

It seemed to me that the girl named Doris didn't really have a chance. She was short and too heavy.

I was glad the one named Tracey had a more casual attitude, since I didn't think she had much chance, either.

She was tall and thin, with sharp cheekbones, but she had such a sloppy look that she didn't stand out among all the gorgeous girls around her.

Tracey shifted her weight from one foot to the other. "Listen, Doris, being a model is dumb. Any bubblehead can stand around like a geek in clothes. You don't want to —"

"I don't want to hear this speech one more time," Doris cried, covering her ears. "I'm not listening to you." She hiccuped twice more and then shut her eyes as if to block Tracey out altogether.

Tracey shook her head. "This is crazy," she muttered to herself. At that moment, she noticed me. It was clear from my interested expression that I'd been listening. "Can I ask you a question?" she said to me. "What's the big deal about being a model? I don't get it."

I opened my mouth to speak, but Kathy, who'd been listening, too, jumped in before I could utter a sound. "What's not to get? Wouldn't you love to wear great clothes, travel, have everyone admire you, and get paid gobs of money for it?"

Tracey looked at Kathy for a moment. At least I assumed she was looking at Kathy from behind those creepy dark glasses. Then she blew a big pink gum bubble and let it snap. "The gobs of money part is cool, I suppose," she said slowly.

Doris took her hands from her ears and smiled. "Tracey thinks this is the dumbest thing. She doesn't realize that this is the chance of a lifetime."

"If it's so dumb, why are you here?" Kathy challenged Tracey.

Tracey hooted with laughter and adjusted her glasses on her delicate, slightly upturned nose. "Not because I want to be a model, that's for sure. I'm keeping Doris company."

"She's my cousin," Doris added as an explanation.

The line was moving forward more quickly than I expected. Standing on tiptoe, I saw that as each girl reached the front of the line she filled out a form and then went to talk to three people—two women and a man—at the center of the table. When they were done, some of the girls went into Just Juniors, a clothing store behind the table. Other girls left, looking disappointed.

"Tracey, listen," I heard Doris say. "When we get to the table and they interview you, don't tell them we're cousins, okay? They might think it's unfair to pick two cousins and they won't—"

"Hold on a minute!" Tracey said, jumping back in alarm. "I told you I'd stand in line with you. That's all, though. I'm not kidding. I'm not trying out for some stupid modeling contest."

"You said you'd stay with me," Doris wailed.

"Yeah, but I'm not entering the contest!"

Although Doris begged and pleaded, Tracey just kept shaking her head. Finally I couldn't stand it anymore. Doris sounded so desperate that I felt sorry for her. "What have you got to lose?" I said, butting in. "Do it for a goof."

Tracey pushed her sunglasses down her nose and gave

me a mind-your-own-business glare. The look was even more shocking because of her eyes. They were a stunning aqua blue. Her pupils looked black and piercing against the light color. They were the most beautiful eyes I'd ever seen.

Despite her glare, Tracey gave in. "Oh, all right. I'm not doing anything today, anyway."

The line kept moving forward quickly as girls went to the table in groups of five. "Knock 'em dead," said Dee when my turn came. I nodded anxiously as I glanced around at the other four girls going to the table with me. They were so beautiful I felt like a troll.

At the table we filled out our forms and then, one at a time, we were interviewed by three judges. One judge was a petite blonde with a clipboard. The attractive woman beside her was in her forties. She had short, stylish brown hair, and she wore a great red suit. She had huge brown eyes. I could tell she was someone important just from the way she acted, like you'd imagine a queen would—confident and in charge. The man on her other side was thin and had blond hair. He smiled and seemed very friendly.

When they asked, I told them that I was doing fine in school and I thought modeling would be fun. I'd probably use the money to go to college, though I also wanted a CD player of my own, so I might skim a bit off for that.

Then they asked me a few more questions. Did I smoke? No! Was I afraid to fly on an airplane? No, I thought flying would be exciting, even though I'd never flown before. Did I have any allergies? No.

When they were done, each of them scribbled something on index cards. The man and the blond-haired woman handed their cards to the queen. "I agree," she said to them. She looked up at me. "Nicole, you've made it through the first elimination round. You'll be in the fashion show. Only fifty girls will participate in that, so congratulations."

I broke into a big smile. "Thank you," I said.

"Great smile," the man said to the women.

The women nodded in a way that was very encouraging. I turned toward Dee and Kathy, who were waiting off by the side of the table, and gave them a thumbs-up.

They went wild. "All right! All right!" Kathy kept shouting as she punched the air triumphantly. The last thing I saw before I was directed into Just Juniors was Kathy and Dee jumping in the air and high-fiving each other.

Inside Just Juniors, a young woman with her blond hair pulled back in a braid stood by the door. She told me to pick out any outfit for the fashion show. "Casual stuff is to the right, dresses are on the back wall, and help yourself to any accessories off the rack. Come see me when you're done, and I'll write down what you've got so Ms. Calico can read it out during the show."

"Do you mean the head of the Calico agency is actually here?" I gasped.

The young woman pointed through the glass door to the three judges. I could see only their backs as they interviewed Tracey, who was now taking off her sunglasses—and looking pretty unhappy about it, too. "The lady in the red suit is Kate Calico," the woman told me. "Isn't she gorgeous?"

"She sure is," I agreed.

"Hurry up and pick your outfit," the woman said. "There isn't a lot of time to make your selection."

It wasn't hard for me to pick. My eyes immediately went to a beautiful western-style skirt. It had about eight tiers of material in different colors. The skirt was gauzy and seemed to float all around me. I put it together with a light green suede vest over a cream-colored, long-sleeved T-shirt and added a pair of cowboy boots. I went to the counter and loaded on a set of colored plastic bangle bracelets.

The store looked as if it were being destroyed as girls pulled clothing off the racks, tried the outfits on, and then changed their minds.

It worried me a little that I had made my choice so quickly, but there I was, all dressed and ready to go. I was standing around watching the other girls when I felt a sharp tap on my shoulder.

I turned and faced Tracey, who had put her sunglasses back on. "Hi," she said, looking lost.

"They picked you!" I cried happily. "That's great."

"No, it's not," Tracey disagreed. "Doris is completely bummed. They told her to lose ten pounds, get a better haircut, and try again next year."

"That's too bad," I said sincerely, though I wasn't very surprised she hadn't made it.

For a moment, Tracey and I stood together looking around the store full of frantic girls. "This is too crazy," Tracey said, turning toward the door. "I'm getting out of here."

"Wait," I said, not exactly sure why. Maybe just because Tracey was someone I'd already spoken to and I didn't want to feel all alone. "Why don't you keep going? What have you got to lose?"

Tracey shrugged. "This is stupid."

"Are you scared?" I asked.

"Scared?" she scoffed. "That would be the day."

"One of the prizes is a thousand-dollar advance on your first modeling jobs," I pointed out, remembering how the money had interested her.

"A thousand dollars," she repeated. "Mom and I could sure use that."

"So, go pick an outfit."

Tracey blew another pink bubble and snapped it. "I'm not really into clothes. Do you think you could help me?"

"Sure," I replied. "What kind of outfit are you looking for?"

"Something that won't make me look like a completely brain-dead geek," she said.

"All right," I told her. "I think we can mangage that. Come on."

Chapter Two

———◆———

ur next modeling hopeful is Ms. Nicole Wilton," Kate Calico announced to the crowd.

"Good luck," Tracey whispered from behind me.

"Thanks," I whispered back in a choked, scared voice. With shaking hands and Jell-O legs, I stepped out onto the green-felt-lined runway that had been quickly set up in front of Just Juniors.

As I headed toward the end of the T-shaped runway, Ms. Calico spoke into a hand-held microphone and read from the application I'd filled out at the table. "Nicole is thirteen and is in the eighth grade at Thomas Dewey Junior High. She plays the flute and enjoys gymnastics. Nicole dreams of being a veterinarian when she gets older." Then she went on to talk about my outfit, the brands and the fabrics and all.

As I walked the long runway, I barely dared to breathe. I couldn't believe how many people had gathered to see the fashion show. I'd never been in front of such a big crowd in my life.

"Hurrah, Nikki! Go! Go!" Two familiar voices rose out of the crowd. Kathy and Dee stood shouting and smiling up at me from the foot of the runway. That made me break out of the phony smile I'd plastered on my face and smile for real.

Still, despite my private cheering section, I was so scared that it felt as if I were floating instead of walking. But somehow I got out there, turned, and then walked back to the area where the forty-nine other contestants were gathered.

"You did great," Tracey greeted me when I finally returned to the group.

"Could you see how much I was shaking?" I asked her.

"Not at all," she assured me. "You looked cool."

"Thanks," I said, feeling a little better. Tracey didn't seem like the type who would say something just to make you feel good.

"Our next contestant is Ms. Tracey Morris," Kate Calico announced to the crowd.

"I hope nobody I know sees me," Tracey muttered as she brushed past me.

"Wait a minute," I whispered as I grabbed her arm. I plucked her sunglasses from her face. "That's better."

Tracey rolled her gorgeous blue eyes and set out for

the runway. She had on black leggings, a gray ribbed turtleneck sweater, a black leather jacket, and a black brimmed cap. It wasn't an outfit I'd have picked for myself, but on her it looked just right. She had the perfect swagger in her walk to make the look come off.

"Tracey is an eighth grader at Susan B. Anthony Junior High. She is a member of the Physics Club and the county's Gifted and Talented program," Ms. Calico read from Tracey's card. "Her interests include video games, stock car racing, and chess. She hopes to be an astronaut or a race car driver when she gets older."

I laughed to myself as I watched Tracey lope by with long strides. Obviously she hadn't been serious when she filled out that card. I wondered what she'd have written if she was serious. There was something unusual about Tracey that made me want to get to know her better.

There were ten more girls after Tracey—each one of them really pretty in her own way. There was so much competition, it seemed crazy to think I could ever win.

When all the girls had modeled, Kate Calico stepped forward and thanked us all. "As you may know," she said to the crowd, "the five girls whom we have selected will join our Calico juniors division."

All around me, the girls stood tensely. Even the audience stopped talking. I clenched my fists nervously.

"Our first winner is Ms. Caroline Johnson."

The crowd applauded as a slim black girl with lots of cornrow braids stepped forward. Ms. Calico shook her hand and gave her an envelope. Then she directed her to one of five chairs on the platform.

The next girl they picked was about my age. She had thick, wavy brown hair and large brown eyes.

"She's not so hot-looking," Tracey whispered to me casually. She didn't seem at all nervous.

"Our third winner is Ms. Tracey Morris," Ms. Calico announced.

Tracey just sat there. I jabbed her shoulder. "That's you!" I cried excitedly. "You won!"

Tracey stared at me as if she were in a state of shock. "Go!" I said, gently pushing her forward.

Looking stunned, Tracey stumbled up onto the platform like a sleepwalker.

The next girl they selected was blond and blue-eyed. Her name was Susan Lane, and I thought she was pretty. Much prettier than I was.

My heart began to sink. Somehow I had the feeling that the last girl selected wouldn't be me.

Oh, well, I thought. It had been a fun thing to do on a Saturday afternoon. I was trying to keep a positive attitude.

"Our final winner today is Ms. Nicole Wilton," Ms. Calico sang out.

My heart banged in my chest. I had won!

It felt like a dream. I heard people clapping—I heard Kathy and Dee screaming their heads off—and slowly my feet carried me up to the platform. Ms. Calico pressed one of the large prize envelopes into my shaking hand.

She had the other four girls come forward and join me as the crowd clapped and cheered. "Thank you all for coming," Ms. Calico told the crowd with a wave of her hand.

As soon as I stepped off the platform, Dee and Kathy pounced and wrapped me in a hug. "We told you you could do it!" Dee yelled. "This is going to be so wonderful for you!"

"Promise you won't forget the little people who made you what you're about to become," Kathy teased, all smiles.

"There's nothing little about you guys," I said, laughing. "I can't believe this. It's...it's...well, un-believable!"

"Let me see that gorgeous prize package," Dee said eagerly. I handed her the envelope, and she quickly opened it. "Look at all these gift certificates, and...ta-da ...here it is. Your modeling contract!" Her brows furrowed in concentration as she scanned the contract. Then her eyes lit up. "You get your first thousand as soon as a parent signs this and you return it! One thousand dollars! Can you imagine?"

"Can you believe that girl Tracey won, too?" Kathy said incredulously. "It must have been her eyes, although she did look pretty cool in that outfit."

At the mention of Tracey's name, I looked around for her. At first I didn't see her. But then I caught sight of her—locked in a tight hug from her cousin Doris.

Chapter Three

Your parents will be so surprised," Dee said as we rode home from the mall on the T-38 bus.

"Think of it," said Kathy, holding up her hands excitedly. "Their daughter left the house a nobody and is returning... a superstar!"

"Not quite." I laughed.

"All right," Dee said, giving in. "You're on the *road* to superstardom. This will really stun them."

"I hope so," I said, clutching my prize envelope anxiously. My parents had always backed me up in anything I wanted to do —but we'd never discussed modeling. I would be taking them completely by surprise.

"What's wrong?" Dee asked. "You have a funny expression on your face."

"I just hope my parents are cool about this."

"Why wouldn't they be?" Kathy cried.

I shrugged my shoulders. "You know. School, for one thing. They take school very seriously. Anything that interferes with it is out of the question."

"Oh, that," said Dee as if it wasn't any big deal. "Anyone can go to school, but not just anybody gets the chance to be a model with the Calico agency."

"Tell that to my mother," I said.

"I will, if you like," Dee offered. "I'll come with you when you tell her."

"Me, too," Kathy said.

I smiled at them. They were such good friends. We've been together since elementary school. Even though there are other girls we hang out with, the three of us are inseparable. Kathy and Dee stood by me when my dad died while I was in the third grade. And they were there for me as I was getting used to my mom dating again. That was when I was in the fifth grade. Then, when I was in the sixth grade, they listened patiently as I complained endlessly about my new stepsister, Eve. That was right after Mom married Martin.

They've always been true blue, and they still were. But I couldn't take them up on their offer. "Thanks, but I have to do this myself," I said as the bus pulled up to my stop.

"Are you sure you don't want us to come?" asked Dee.

"I'm sure," I said, waving to them. "Wish me luck."

"Luck!" they sang out together.

I walked the five blocks to my house. At first I could

think of it only as Martin's house—the house Mom, my brother, and I moved into two years ago when Martin and Mom got married. Now I thought of it as my home, too.

Martin is a lawyer, and soon my mom will also be one. She's a paralegal now (that's a lawyer's assistant), but she's going to law school at night.

As I walked up the steps, I tried to map out a strategy for breaking the news to Mom and Martin. Nothing came to mind.

"Hi," I called as I went into the living room. There was no answer, but I heard a noise in the kitchen. Mom was sitting at the kitchen table, her long blond curls draped over her face as she studied a fat law book. "Hi," I repeated louder.

Mom almost flipped off her chair. "Oh, Nikki," she gasped, putting her hand over her heart. "You scared me. I didn't hear you come in."

"Sorry," I said. Mom has an amazing ability to block everything else out totally when she's studying. "Interesting stuff?" I asked.

She got up and stirred a pot of tomato sauce that was simmering on the stove. It smelled great. Saturday is the one day of the week when Mom cooks a full-scale supper.

"Interesting? No," she answered. "But I have an exam on it on Tuesday. How was the mall?"

"Exciting," I replied.

Mom tilted her head. "Really? What was so exciting?"

I shifted from foot to foot, then sat down. That felt

wrong, so I stood again. In a tumble of words, I told her about the contest. "You won't believe it, Mom, but...I won!" I finished. "I'm going to be a model!"

She took a step back when I blurted out the last sentence. "Well, congratulations," she said with a smile. "That's great."

"Do you really think so?" I asked eagerly.

Mom sat at the table and looked at me, her brows creased in thought. "Well, of course it's great that you won. But this is all kind of sudden, isn't it?" she said. "I had no idea you wanted to be a model."

"I didn't," I admitted. "Then Kathy and Dee got me thinking about how exciting it would be."

"Are you sure you want to do this?" Mom asked.

I sat down across from her. "Yes. I have to try it, Mom. I can't just walk away from a chance like this. There were over two hundred girls there, and I was one of the ones they picked. Me!"

"You're a beautiful girl, Nikki," Mom said. "That's no surprise. But there's more to you than that. You're bright and athletic. What about your flute lessons and your gymnastics? What about school? You're so young."

"I can still do all those things," I insisted.

Mom shook her head doubtfully. "I don't think modeling is something you can do halfheartedly. It's my impression that you have to make a full-time commitment to it."

"Kate Calico seems like a reasonable person," I said.

"I'm sure she knows we have lives."

A fond smile spread across Mom's face. "When I was about twelve, Kate Calico was *the* top model. She was so beautiful. I wanted to be just like her, with her long, straight brown hair. I scorched my hair once, trying to iron it straight like hers."

"You ironed your hair?" I cried in disbelief.

Mom laughed and nodded. "When that didn't work, I cut the tops and bottoms from soup cans to make huge rollers. I was desperate for straight hair like Kate Calico's."

"Did the soup cans work?" I asked.

"Yes, but it was such a bother. I've always wondered what happened to Kate Calico. She was in a few dumb horror movies, and then she seemed to disappear."

I could *not* picture Kate Calico in a horror movie! However, I couldn't picture Mom walking around with soup cans clipped to her head, either.

Taking the contract out of my prize envelope, I handed it to Mom. "You have to sign this."

The foggy smile left Mom's face. Something about a contract must have brought back the budding lawyer in her. "I don't know about this, Nikki," she said.

I jumped out of the chair. "What do you mean? This is my life, isn't it?"

"Yes, but you're very young."

"I'm thirteen! That's not so young."

"Nikki, I want you to have a balanced, normal life."

Tears sprang to my eyes. "You want me to stay a baby!" I shouted.

Just then I heard the front door close. "Hey, it smells good in here!" cried Todd, practically flying into the kitchen. "What's cooking?"

"Oh, it's a…a…tomato sauce," Mom stammered. "How was the soccer game?"

"We won." Todd is ten and old enough to know when something's up. "You guys look all bent out of shape. What's the matter?"

Before Mom could answer, Martin walked into the kitchen. I looked at him hopefully. Martin and I usually see things the same way. Even though he's only been my stepdad for a little over two years, he and I hit it off from the start. "Don't you think I'm old enough to be a model, Martin? You do, don't you?"

Martin looked confused. He rubbed his hand across the balding top of his head. "Well, sure. I guess so. What exactly are we talking about?"

"A model?" Todd hooted with laughter. "What are you going to model? Halloween costumes? You could be the Bride of Frankenstein."

"Quiet, dweeb," I shot back. "Nobody asked you!"

"Would someone tell me what's going on?" Martin asked helplessly.

"Nikki has just gone out and won a modeling contract," Mom said.

"Is that so?" said Martin. He sounded delighted.

"That's wonderful, kiddo. Good going!"

"Martin," Mom said firmly. "I agree that it's wonderful that she won, but I'm not so sure this is the best thing for Nikki at this stage of her life."

"You're not?" Martin questioned, the smile fading from his broad face.

"Martin!" I cried. "Tell her she's wrong."

"Listen, kiddo, maybe your mother and I should take a moment alone to talk this out," he said.

A moment alone! That was bad news. I knew Mom would win. Martin always lets her have the last word when it comes to me and Todd. He has the final say with Eve. It has something to do with who is the stepparent and who is the biological parent.

Suddenly I felt tears welling in my eyes. I had to get out of there. Brushing past Martin and Todd, I ran out of the kitchen and up the stairs to my bedroom. I flung myself on the bed. This was unbelievable! The greatest thing imaginable had happened to me, and my mother was saying no, I couldn't do it.

And then—as if things weren't bad enough—Eve came in.

I've tried to like Eve, who turned seventeen recently. Believe me, I've tried! But Eve isn't an easy person to like. She's just a lump. She's overweight and couldn't care less about her looks.

That would be all right with me, except that her personality is worse than her looks. She's supposed to be really smart. But other than her superior attitude, I've never seen her display any signs of great genius.

Worst of all, I've never seen her do one nice thing for anyone. Not even her own father, whom she doesn't get along with particularly well.

For example, any dope could tell I was upset, but Eve didn't seem to notice. And even a stranger would have asked me what was wrong. Instead, Eve took a book off her dresser and plopped on her bed to read it.

It was hard to cry with her lying there like that, so I sat up on the edge of the bed. As annoying as Eve is, I wanted someone to talk to. For a moment, I considered confiding in her.

Then I thought better of it. The last time I'd tried that was when I asked her why a boy I liked in school didn't notice me. She'd told me it was probably because I was pretty uninteresting. It wasn't a help.

After a minute, I got up to leave.

"I wouldn't go down there," Eve advised, without looking up from her book.

"Why?"

"Dad and your mother are having a big conversation about your future as a model. Strategically I don't think it would be beneficial to interrupt them at this juncture. It could tilt things out of your favor."

"You mean it's in my favor now?" I asked hopefully.

Eve shrugged. "You know Dad. *You* can't do anything wrong in his eyes. Plus he wants you to like him, so he's trying to convince your mother that modeling is not a completely degrading pursuit—which, of course, it is."

"What's degrading about it?" I challenged angrily.

"You mean, besides the fact that anyone with the brain of a chimp could do it? If you want to stand around like a human dummy, it's none of my business," she said, going back to her book.

I quickly stuck out my tongue at Eve. I know it's childish, but making faces at Eve is a good way to let off some steam.

I sat there for a while, not sure what to do. I looked over at the poster of my pretend boyfriend, Mark, which hung over my bed. His blue eyes were warm beneath his blond curls as he smiled down at me, his surfboard tucked under his arm.

I should explain that I've never met Mark. That's probably not even his name. He's just a guy on a poster. One day Dee and I were complaining that neither of us has ever had a boyfriend, so we went down to the Poster Express and each bought a poster of a cute guy. We were in a goofy mood and decided to pretend the guys were our boyfriends.

Anyway, I looked up at Mark, and his smile made me feel a little better. It was as if he were on my side.

Wiping my eyes one more time, I left the room and headed to the top of the stairs, hoping I'd be able to hear some of Mom and Martin's conversation.

"She won't have time for anything else!" Mom said

heatedly from the living room below.

"You don't know that," Martin countered calmly. "Why not see how it pans out?"

"Because she's my daughter!" Mom shouted. "I can't take chances with her future!"

Their voices dropped and I couldn't hear them anymore. Carefully I crept down two more steps.

I guess I wouldn't make much of a spy. Instantly Mom walked over to the stairs. "Why don't you come down and join the conversation?" Mom suggested.

"All right," I agreed. My heart pounding, I went downstairs.

"Listen," Mom said, taking my hand. "Maybe I'm overly protective. It's not because I want to ruin your life—it's because you are so precious to me. I want what's best for you."

"Modeling isn't bad for me," I said, working hard to be calm and reasonable.

"We see that there's a phone number on this contract," Martin pointed out. "Your mother and I would like to call Ms. Calico and speak to her ourselves. Is that all right with you?"

"Sure!"

"Then, if we're satisfied that it sounds like a good thing for you, we'll sign the contract."

"All right!" I cheered. Ms. Calico was so charming, I was positive she'd win Mom and Martin over in a minute. I was on my way!

Chapter Four

——◆——

If you want life to start moving in slow motion, try waiting for something really exciting to happen. That's how it was waiting for Monday to come so Mom could call Ms. Calico.

But *finally* Monday arrived. My first-period English class was over at nine-fifteen. As soon as I walked out, I raced down to the phone booth in the school lobby and called Mom at her office. "Did you call yet?"

"Yes," she said. "And Ms. Calico was very reassuring. I think it will be fine."

"Yes!" I cried, doing a little dance of joy right there in the phone booth.

"She says that your schoolwork won't suffer if you make a commitment not to let it," Mom said pointedly. "I expect that commitment, Nikki."

"Absolutely, Mom! You can count on me."

"All right. I'll hold you to that. Ms. Calico says you should go to see your guidance counselor as soon as possible."

"Why?" I asked.

"You'll need to rearrange your schedule so that most of your classes are in the morning. That way you'll be freer to work in the afternoon."

"That makes sense, I guess," I agreed. "Thanks, Mom."

"Okay, sweetheart. I just put the signed contract in the office mail. Ms. Calico wants to see you tomorrow at four."

"Tomorrow!" I shrieked excitedly. "Tomorrow!"

"Is something wrong with tomorrow?" Mom asked.

"It's just so...so...soon."

"I'm not sure how you're going to get there," said Mom. "I have that big exam tomorrow, and I won't get back in time for it if I drive you. I'm not sure what Martin's schedule is like. We'll figure it out tonight."

"Thanks again," I said. "See you tonight."

Just then there was a knock on the glass of the phone booth. It was Dee. "There you are!" she said. "I've been looking all over for you. Come on, we're going to be late."

She and I had a study hall with Mr. Eagleton next period. He's the only study hall monitor in the whole school who gives detention for lateness. Dee and I began jogging toward the room. Breathlessly I told her about the conversation I'd just had with my mother. "And Ms. Calico wants to see me tomorrow!" I said.

Dee skidded to a stop. "You can't go tomorrow!"

"Why not?"

"Did you forget about the planning meeting for the Oktoberfest Dance tomorrow?" she asked.

I put my hand over my mouth. I had forgotten—though I didn't know how I could have. Kathy, Dee, and I had decided that we'd be on the planning committee as soon as it was announced. Back in August, we'd made a pact to be the most involved, active students this school had ever seen. We were going to be doers, not watchers.

"What should I do?" I asked Dee. "I'll have to call and say I can't see Ms. Calico tomorrow."

"Don't you dare!" she cried. "I want my limo ride."

Suddenly, Kathy came hurrying down the hall. "What are you guys standing here for?" she asked without slowing down. She grabbed my arm and began dragging me along. "We are a split second away from detention-ville."

At once all of us broke into a full run, slipping and sliding on the polished floor. We swung around the corner and slid through the half-open door just as Mr. Eagleton was closing it. "Nice of you ladies to join us," he said snidely as we rushed past him.

"Sorry," I panted. "But we're here now."

"So you are," he said, arching an eyebrow. "Please take your seats."

Kathy and Dee took seats together in the back corner of the classroom. I sat in the one remaining seat, about four seats over. When I glanced at them, I saw that they were whispering and looking my way. Looking down at my math book, I tried to concentrate, but it was hard.

In a couple of minutes, a note came sliding onto my desk from the girl next to me. It said: *We'll tell the committee you want to work on Oktoberfest but just couldn't make the first meeting. We'll say you were sick. Okay? K & D.*

I smiled at them and gave a thumbs up. They were so great.

Then, since I couldn't think about math, anyway, I decided it would be a good time to talk to my guidance counselor, Ms. Turnbull, about changing my schedule. I went up and asked Mr. Eagleton if I could go. He looked at me suspiciously, but he wrote out a pass.

As I headed for the door, I saw Kathy and Dee looking questioningly at me. Since there was no way I could tell them where I was going, I just smiled and gave a little wave.

Down in the guidance office, I had to wait about ten minutes to see Ms. Turnbull. She's a very petite woman in her fifties with short gray hair. Ms. Turnbull doesn't really seem like the type who could possibly *guide* anyone, but she's been with the school for about a million years, so I suppose she knows what she's doing.

"Come in, Michelle," she said, walking to the door of the outside office.

"Nicole," I corrected her politely.

"Oh, sorry. Nicole, of course. Excuse me." Ms.

Turnbull sat at her desk and opened my file. "What can I do for you?"

"I need to rearrange my schedule if that's possible."

Ms. Turnbull pursed her lips and shook her head doubtfully. "These schedules were made well in advance. There isn't much room for flexibility. I'm afraid I can't—"

"Please," I begged. "I've just received a contract to be a model, and if I can't move my classes, then I can't—"

"A model!" Ms. Turnbull gasped. "How thrilling!" Then her eyes narrowed. "Is that the truth?"

"Yes, honestly. I entered the model search contest at the mall over the weekend." Ms. Turnbull still looked doubtful, so I added, "I can bring a note from my mother, if you want."

That seemed to do the trick. Ms. Turnbull took a copy of my schedule from her folder and sat forward. "A note will be fine. Let's see what we can work out for you."

I was impressed. Just the mere mention of my future modeling career had gotten a whole different reaction from Ms. Turnbull. Was this how it was going to be from now on? Was everything going to be easier because people were impressed with my modeling?

Ms. Turnbull took me out of my afternoon history class and switched me into Ms. Snyder's history class, which was held during what used to be my morning study hall. That was all right. The really bad part was that I had to switch out of my last-period math class into Mr. Eagleton's morning class. Everyone knew Mr. Eagleton was the hardest math teacher in the school, and math has always been my most difficult subject. I also had to drop an art class that I really liked. But I had no choice.

With no study halls and no lunch, I could be out every day by one-thirty. That was the best she could do, so it would have to be good enough. "Thank you, Ms. Turnbull," I said, getting up from my seat. "I appreciate your help a lot."

"You're quite welcome, dear," she replied, handing me a copy of my new schedule. "You can begin this tomorrow, as soon as you bring me that note from your mother. We want you to have every opportunity to do well in your exciting new career. Good luck. And come see me if you have any problems."

"I will. Thanks again."

I got back to study hall just as the bell rang for the end of the period. "Where did you go?" Dee asked, rushing up to me right away.

Her jaw dropped when I told Kathy and her about rearranging my schedule. "You won't be in history with me anymore!" Dee said unhappily.

"You'll have Eagleton for math!" Kathy moaned. "What a nightmare."

"And you won't be able to eat lunch with us, either," added Kathy. "We've *always* eaten lunch together."

"You guys!" I cried. "You were the ones who talked me into doing this. Remember?"

"I know, but what about Oktoberfest?" said Dee. "The

planning meetings start at three o'clock. You'll be long gone by then."

"Listen," I told them. "I'm not going to the city every single day. This just means I *can* leave if I have to. Otherwise, I'll stick around and do my homework until three if there's something going on after school. I can even eat with you for the second half of lunch."

"You're right, you're right," Dee said sulkily. "I just didn't think so much would change if you became a model."

Kathy gave her a strong shove on the shoulder. "Nothing is really changing. Give her a break."

"She's right. Nothing will change," I said, putting my hand on Dee's shoulder. "Come on, we have to get to our last history class together."

Dee smiled at me. "I hear Snyder is much easier than Ms. Barbero."

"Yeah, but nothing makes up for getting Eagleton," Kathy sighed as we walked down the hall together.

That afternoon when I got home, the only one there was Todd. He was already deeply involved in Super Nintendo, his favorite thing on earth. "Hi, Squirt," I said as I came in and tossed my books on the stairs.

"Don't call me that," he said, blowing a battleship to smithereens. The word *Win!* blinked on and off in big red letters on the screen. "Nikki," he said, turning away from the television, "when you become a model, are you going to do embarrassing stuff like appear in your underwear or anything like that?"

I hadn't thought about it. "I don't think so," I told him.

"Good, because I wouldn't want to have to quit school or move or anything. Especially not now when my soccer team is tied for first place in the league."

"I don't think you have to worry," I said, climbing the stairs.

Mom and Martin pulled into the driveway at about five-thirty. I ran down to greet them. "Hi," I said cheerfully. "How was work?"

"Busy," said Mom, looking tired.

"Aggravating," said Martin as he put down his briefcase.

That didn't sound encouraging, but I launched into my next question, anyway. "So, Martin, can you take me into the city tomorrow?"

Martin looked at my mother in confusion. "What's tomorrow?"

"Nikki needs to see Ms. Calico tomorrow in the city at four," Mom explained. "But I have a big exam. I was hoping maybe you could . . ."

Martin slowly shook his head. "I'm really sorry. I have a closing on a piece of commercial real estate. There's no way I can miss it."

"No problem," I quickly replied. "I can take the train."

"I don't think so," Mom disagreed. "You're too young."

"I'm not too young to buy a train ticket and sit there for a half hour and then get off at the end of the line," I argued.

"I said no," Mom insisted calmly.

I opened my mouth to argue some more, but then I shut it, deciding not to push my luck. The three of us stood looking at one another, not knowing what to do.

At that moment, Eve came winging in the front door. There was something very different about her. She wasn't wearing her usual grumpy expression. In fact, she looked absolutely thrilled. "Ta-da!" she sang out, holding up a slip of white paper.

"You passed your driver's test!" Mom said happily.

"Hey, Eve, does that mean you can finally move that wreck you bought out of the garage so I can get my bike in and out?" asked Todd, popping up from the television set.

"That's right," said Eve. "I am now a licensed driver! I can drive anywhere, anytime."

Martin's face brightened. "Hey, this solves our problem. Eve has had lessons in city driving. She can drive Nikki to the city!"

I swallowed hard. I sure didn't like the sound of *that!* Owing Eve for such a big favor could only mean bad news for me.

Chapter Five

———◆———

Watch where you're going, you moron!" Eve screamed at the driver she'd just cut off as we swerved into a gas station on the corner of a city block. I scrunched as far down in the seat as I possibly could. Driving with Eve was like being stuck inside one of Todd's video games. Eve's goal seemed to be to crash into everything she saw, although I have to admit she hadn't hit a car, sign, or curb yet.

"You have two choices," Eve told me. "You can pay to have super unleaded put into my car, or you can save a little money and pump it yourself."

I chose to pump it myself since I only had twenty dollars of my baby-sitting money with me. After I figured out how to use the pump and got grease on my hands and dribbled gas down the front of my denim jacket, we were finally on our way again.

By the time Eve pulled up in front of the modern chrome and glass building of the Calico Modeling Agency, I was a basket case. "Be back here at six o'clock sharp," Eve said as I staggered out of the car. "If you're not, I'm leaving. And don't tell your mother that I didn't come up with you or I'll never take you in again."

"Yes, Eve, darling," I said sarcastically.

"Don't get wise with me. Remember, you need me." As if Eve hadn't been bad enough before, driving had now made her power-crazed.

"See you at six," I said, closing the door behind me. With a screech of tires, Eve zoomed off to further terrify unsuspecting pedestrians and drivers.

I stood and looked up at the building. It was so tall, it hurt my neck to try to see the top. Taking a deep breath, I went through the revolving door and into the lobby.

The Calico Modeling Agency was on the ninth floor. When I stepped out of the elevator, I saw the name Calico written in gold letters over a wide, arched doorway. It was kind of hard to miss.

Classical music filled the air as I stepped through the archway onto the plush, sea green carpet. Out front was a curved reception desk that was so polished it seemed to shine. After my cyclone ride with Eve, I felt like Dorothy entering the Emerald City.

On the walls were posters of models—women so lovely they could hardly be real. Sitting on the green leather couches were stunning, perfectly groomed young women clutching leather folders. Suddenly I felt like a klutzy kid, all arms and legs.

"May I help you?" the receptionist asked politely, but with a brisk edge to her voice. She looked me up and down with her heavily made-up eyes.

"I'm Nicole Wilton. Um…I'm…um…here to see Ms. Calico," I stammered nervously. "I have an appointment."

The receptionist checked the big appointment book on her desk. Then she punched in some numbers and told Ms. Calico's secretary I was there. "Take a seat," she said to me after a moment. "Ms. Calico's assistant, Renata Marco, will be with you shortly."

All the young women on the couches looked at me. I guess they were wondering why I had an appointment with Ms. Calico—the queen, herself. I wondered why they were all sitting there.

In a few minutes, Renata Marco came out into the reception area. I recognized her right away, since she'd been one of the contest judges. Today she looked like a petite gypsy in a gauzy, flowered dress and very high-heeled shoes with thick straps at the ankles. All the young women on the couches sat forward, looking at her attentively, but Renata didn't pay any attention to them. Instead she smiled warmly at me. "Hi, Nikki," she greeted me. "Please come this way."

Clutching my hands together nervously, I followed her down a long, carpeted hall. "Who are all those girls out there?" I asked.

"We're having an open call today," Renata explained. "Those young women have all brought their portfolios, hoping the agency will sign them."

"What's a portfolio?" I asked.

"It's a book full of pictures photographers have taken of them," Renata answered. "You'll have to get one, too."

"How do I do that?"

Renata pushed open a heavy wooden door. "Kate will tell you all about it," she said. We stepped into a sunny office with shiny wood paneling and lots of plants. Ms. Calico got up from behind her big desk. She was dressed in another great suit. This one was a deep cobalt blue.

"Welcome to the Calico Modeling Agency," she said, shaking my hand. It made me feel very sophisticated.

We sat down and talked about a few different things. Then Ms. Calico explained how I would go about putting together my portfolio. My prize package contained three hundred-dollar gift certificates. Those certificates would be honored by any of ten photographers on a list that was also in my package. "Normally girls have to lay out their own money to get these shots taken," said Ms. Calico, "but the three hundred dollars should pretty much cover—"

Just then the door to the office flew open. A very pretty girl about my age with bouncy blond curls and big brown eyes ran into the room. Although I wasn't sure why, she looked familiar. "Kate, I'm sorry to interrupt, but she's done it to me again!" the girl cried. "I tell her and tell her, but she won't listen."

"Who's done what, Ashley, dear?" Ms. Calico asked.

"Rose Marie!" Ashley exploded. "She's booked me over at GirlTogs again. And I won't work for them. She knows that, but for some reason she insists on booking me there."

Ms. Calico frowned. "As I recall, you had some difficulty with the photographer there."

"He hates my nose. He says that if he doesn't shoot it exactly right, it comes out looking like a pig snout." Her nose looked perfectly fine to me, although it was sort of squared off at the tip and slightly upturned. "If he doesn't like the way I have my head tilted, he oinks like a pig to get me to change position."

"Oh, dear, that is uncalled for," Ms. Calico sympathized. "What's his name again?"

"John Puddingham," Ashley huffed, crossing her arms.

"Excuse me for a moment," Ms. Calico said, turning to me. As she punched in some numbers on her phone, I remembered where I'd seen the girl before. She was on the back cover of one of Mom's magazines, in an ad for a new spaghetti sauce. The girl in front of me had been smiling and holding up a forkful of spaghetti and sauce.

"Yes, hello, Tom," Ms. Calico said to someone on the other end. "I have a small problem I hope you can help me with." She spoke in warm, friendly terms, but by the end of the conversation, Ms. Calico had gotten a new photographer assigned to the GirlTogs account.

"It's all set, Ashley," Ms. Calico told her. "By the way,

I'd like you to meet Nikki Wilton. She'll be joining us. Nikki, this is Ashley Taylor, one of our most popular models."

"Hi," I said. "I've seen you in a spaghetti sauce ad."

"Oh, that tacky thing," Ashley scoffed. "I look like such a twerp in that!"

"Nonsense," said Ms. Calico. "You were called back twice by the Pastaperfect company."

"I guess I have the kind of face that sells spaghetti," Ashley said. Then her smile faded. "Does that mean I have a fat face?"

"No, dear, you have a healthy, fat-free carbohydrate glow," Ms. Calico assured her.

Ashley's smile returned.

At that moment, an Asian girl stuck her head in the doorway. Her short black hair was cut in a wedge shape with long bangs. She smiled and waved at Ms. Calico. "Hi, Ms. C." She then turned to Ashley. "Are you going over to GirlTogs or not?" she asked. "The cab is waiting for us."

Ms. Calico introduced me to Chloe Chang. "Hello," she said, eyeing me cautiously.

The way she looked at me made me uncomfortable. "Hello," I said.

"Girls," Ms. Calico said to Ashley and Chloe, "I've set up a test shoot for Nikki. It's in the same building as GirlTogs. Take her over there with you, would you please?"

"Sure thing," said Ashley. "Come on, Nikki, we'll show you the ropes."

"Good-bye, Ms. Calico," I said as I stood up to leave.

"Good-bye, Nikki," she said. "Good luck on your first shoot."

I followed Ashley and Chloe out into the hall. "Hold on a sec," said Ashley as she ducked into an office where Renata sat behind her desk.

"This is so exciting," I said to Chloe.

"Yes, I suppose it is," she said, not really looking at me. "I was only eight when I went on my first shoot, so I don't really remember."

Ashley came bouncing out of Renata's office. "Renata says a strong and positive new influence is coming into my life today. But Mars has also moved into my house of communication, which, of course, is terrible. I'll have to be sure to communicate my head off so there are no misunderstandings."

"That shouldn't be any problem for you." Chloe laughed.

"Are you saying I talk too much?" Ashley asked, pretending to be offended.

"You? Never!" Chloe teased.

I hurried after Ashley and Chloe as they went down the hall. "You must think I'm nuts, Nikki, but I really do believe in horoscopes," Ashley told me.

"Did Renata read yours in the newspaper?" I asked.

"Read it!" Ashley gasped. "Oh, no. Renata is a real

astrologer. She's done my chart based on my time of birth as well as my birthday. I check in with her every day for a reading."

"Wow!" I said. "Do you really believe all that?"

"Of course!" cried Ashley. "Renata knows all that stuff. She's a palm reader, a numerologist, an aura reader—you name it. She's great."

We breezed through the lobby where all the modeling hopefuls were still anxiously waiting. At the end of the couch I saw Tracey, wearing black jeans, a black sweater, and her sunglasses. "Hey, hi," I said.

"Hi," Tracey replied. "Are you here to—"

"Come on, the cab is waiting," Ashley interrupted, pulling me out the door by my wrist.

"Bye!" I called to Tracey with an apologetic smile.

"Sorry to be rude," said Ashley. "But these photographers get all huffy if you're late. And you can't be late for your very first shoot. You've got to get off to a good start. That's very important."

We rode down the elevator, watching the red numbers flash by. Suddenly Ashley turned to me. "Hey! Maybe you're the important new influence in my life."

"Gee, I don't know," I stammered.

"Yes, of course, you must be. Nothing else new has happened to me so far. You must be it!"

"I bought you that book about acting," said Chloe as we went through the crowded lobby. "That could be a new influence."

"No, no," Ashley disagreed, weaving around people at a fast clip. "It's Nikki. I can feel it."

I smiled and shrugged my shoulders at Chloe. Somehow it seemed best to make light of it all. But Chloe didn't respond. She just frowned deeply, a hurt expression on her face.

Chapter Six

—————•————

No!" said Ashley in a shocked voice. "I can't believe you've never been in a cab before."

"It's true," I admitted, feeling childish and unsophisticated compared to Ashley and Chloe. "This is my first cab ride."

"Can you imagine that, Chloe?" Ashley asked.

Chloe just shrugged. I wondered if she felt threatened by all the attention Ashley was paying to me. I didn't want to hurt her feelings, but I couldn't control Ashley. It didn't seem to me that anyone could.

"Chloe and I spend half our lives in cabs," said Ashley. "In fact, I was born in a cab!"

"What?" I said skeptically.

"It's true. My mother was a weather reporter on TV in St. Louis at the time, and she started having contractions while she was on the air. So she just waited and waited until her weather report was over, and then she went and got a cab. But the cab got stuck in traffic, so I was born right there," Ashley explained. "That's Mom for you. She doesn't let anything get in the way of her career, not even having a baby."

"Gee, I was born in a boring old hospital," I said. "Is your mom still on TV?"

"Oh, yes. I'm sure you've seen her. She's Taylor Andrews."

"Taylor Andrews!" I cried. "You don't mean Taylor Andrews from 'Breakfast with Taylor,' do you?"

"That's her," said Ashley.

Now that I looked at her closely, Ashley did look a lot like the perky blond talk show host. I really liked Taylor Andrews. She seemed so smart and stylish. I couldn't believe I was sitting with her daughter.

"Chloe was born in her own home," Ashley said as the cab slowed to a stop at a light.

"Couldn't your mother get to the hospital in time, either?" I asked. Maybe traffic was always so bad in cities that no one ever got to the hospital.

"My grandmother used to be a midwife in China," Chloe said. "She'd delivered lots of babies, so she helped."

"Chloe is lucky. She lives downtown with her entire family in this great building they own," said Ashley. "Her grandparents live on the floor above her, and her aunt and uncle live on the floor above them. And they have this great restaurant on the ground floor. They serve the best food you've ever eaten in your life."

"It's okay," Chloe murmured. What was with her? Maybe she was just shy when she met new people.

The cab pulled to the curb on a busy side street. Ashley paid as Chloe and I climbed out. I followed Ashley and Chloe into the lobby of a plain, narrow building. Ashley hit a button and a loud buzzer went off. "Come on," she said, pulling open an inner door.

"Where's the elevator?" I asked, looking around.

"It's always broken," Ashley said. "This building is a pain. You have to walk up."

By the time we got to the seventh floor, I was huffing and puffing. "This is where you go," said Ashley, jerking her thumb toward one of two doors on the floor. "Chloe and I have to go up to GirlTogs on eight. Good luck."

"Thanks," I answered. As Chloe and Ashley continued up the steps, I hovered anxiously outside the door. I needed a moment to work up the nerve to pull that door open. I just didn't know what to expect.

"What's the matter?" Ashley called down to me.

"I'm a little scared, I guess."

She looked at Chloe and then back down at me. "Chloe, tell them I'll be right up, okay?"

"Ashley," Chloe grumbled. "They expect both of us."

"You go first. I'll be there before you're done," Ashley insisted.

As Ashley climbed down the stairs to me, Chloe threw her arms into the air. She let out a long, exasperated breath and continued going up.

"Chloe hates to break the rules," Ashley whispered to me. "But I believe that's what rules are for. Chloe's never late, always prepared, but I say, let them wait. If you act like you're hot stuff, that's how you get treated. Come on, let's get you set up in here."

Ashley yanked open the door, and we stepped into a high-ceilinged studio. In the middle of the room was a large piece of blue paper set up on poles as a backdrop. Standing in front of the backdrop was a beautiful model. Off to the right, a large electric fan blew her long blond hair and silky dress behind her. A man in a T-shirt and jeans danced around the set, snapping pictures of the model as she constantly moved, striking one pose after another.

Abruptly he stopped. "Okay, that's the end of my roll. I think we have some good stuff to show them. It's a wrap."

A girl with short purple hair, dressed in a black jumpsuit, approached us. "Hi, Nia," Ashley said. "This is Nikki. She's here for—"

"Test shots, right?" Nia said. "I know. I talked to Kate myself. I'll be right back." She hurried over to the photographer and left us standing together.

Off to one side of the room was a vanity table with lights all around the mirror. "Where's your makeup bag?" Ashley asked me.

"I don't have one," I said. "I don't usually wear makeup. And Ms. Calico told me she wanted a natural look, so I didn't think I should wear any today."

Ashley shook her head. "No, no, no! There's natural pretty and natural blah. Without makeup, your face will disappear under those harsh lights." She nodded toward the bright lights on high poles that shone on either side of the stage-like setting.

"Sit down," she said, pulling out the vanity stool for me. As I sat, Ashley took a red plastic case from the large canvas bag she was carrying. She uncapped mascara and did my lashes. "Yow-ee, you have long lashes once you color the blond ends," she noted. "You should always wear mascara." Then she applied some blush to my cheekbones with a soft, fat brush and put tinted gloss on my lips. "There," she said, satisfied. "Now you look natural and good. You might need a little eyeliner, but wait and see how the photos come out."

"Thanks," I said.

"You're welcome. Good thing I came in with you."

"That's true," I said with a smile. "Have you been doing this a long time?"

"Practically since I was born," she answered, proudly tossing her blond curls over her shoulder. "I was a Tasty Tots baby and I just kept going from there."

Just then the photographer approached. "Are you ready?" he asked me.

"Nikki, this is Allan Morgan," Ashley said, introducing us. "Be patient with her, Allan. This is her first time out."

Allan gave her a smile. "If you say so, Ashley. You're my girl."

Ashley smiled back at him. "Allan is the best," she told me. "I've worked with him a zillion times. He gets pictures like nobody else."

"Is that what you're wearing?" Allan asked me. From the tone of his voice, I knew he didn't think my long-sleeved yellow T-shirt and black, pleated skirt were a good idea.

"No good?" I asked.

"Not particularly interesting," said Allan, squinting his eyes as though he were deep in thought.

"How about one of those bathing suits from the shoot we did last week?" Ashley suggested.

"Good idea. They're over there," Allan said, pointing across the room. "You can pick one."

Ashley took hold of my wrist. "Come on. I know just the perfect one for you." She led me to a rack on the far side of the studio, by the window. Ashley's hand went right to a navy blue one-piece suit with a gold anchor on the front and a ruffled gold skirt at the hips. "This is you," she said.

She rummaged in a cardboard box beside the rack and pulled out a shiny gold sailor hat. "This will finish it perfectly. And, look, there are some gold sandals here, too." Pulling the sandals from the box, she steered me toward a screen set up in a corner. "Get dressed behind there."

Luckily the suit fit perfectly. Plunking the sailor hat on my head, I stepped out from behind the screen.

Ashley immediately tugged the hat forward and to the side. "Gorgeous," she announced, stepping back.

Allan and Nia, his purple-haired assistant, were draping a big roll of yellow paper over the blue paper they had been using. I guessed that was what I would be standing in front of.

"No, no, use the ocean one!" Ashley cried, running over to them excitedly. "The one you used for Chloe the other day. She showed me the proofs of that shoot. It looked super."

Allan sighed good-naturedly. "Get the shore scene, please, Nia."

Nia lugged a long roll of paper over from the corner of the room. Together she and Allan draped it over the backdrop stand. It showed a beach and waves washing up to the shore under a sunny, blue sky. "Excellent," Ashley said, giggling happily. "This will look so cool in your book, Nikki." With a gentle shove, she pushed me toward the backdrop. "Go on, have fun at the beach. I've got to rush up to GirlTogs."

I took my place on the paper, trying not to look as nervous and awkward as I felt. Allan held his camera up. "All right, Nikki, hon, toss your hair back and give me a big smile."

Taking a deep breath, I tossed my hair and pushed the corners of my mouth up into a smile.

"Try to smile with your eyes," Allan coached me. I had no idea what he was talking about. "Drop those shoulders and take a deep breath," he said patiently. "You're too tense."

We tried some more shots, but from Allan's serious

expression, I could sense it wasn't going well. "You're not relaxing," Allan said softly.

"Okay, I'm relaxed now," I said. "Really."

I guess I didn't look too relaxed, however. "Loosen up. This isn't torture," Allan said with a pleasant laugh. He could have fooled me. I'd never done anything more torturous. I felt completely foolish. No matter which way I moved, it felt all wrong.

Before this day, I'd always considered the worst event of my life to be when I fell off the balance beam in front of the entire school during sports night. That incident had now moved to second place. *This* was the new first-place winner for most humiliating event.

After forty-five minutes, Allan stopped snapping shots. "Are we all done?" I asked wearily.

"Almost," he said. "Go change back into your regular clothes. I'll get a couple of shots of you wearing that. Then we'll do a couple of head shots and we'll be finished."

"All right," I agreed, glad to walk out of the hot lights. As I gathered my clothes from a chair, the studio door opened. Nia came in with a teenage boy.

My heart slammed into my chest. I knew the boy. Well, not exactly, but I had his picture on my bedroom wall. He was Mark, the guy with the surfboard, the mystery love of my life!

Just then I heard a gentle click. Turning toward the sound, I saw that Allan had snapped a picture of me. "A candid," he explained with a shrug.

The guy I called Mark had been talking to Nia, but suddenly he looked in my direction. "That's Jim Corcoran," said Allan. "He starts billing me in ten minutes, so let's get moving."

I hurried behind the screen and quickly changed. When I came out, Allan had moved a scruffy armchair near the window. "Just sit and we'll finish up this roll," he said.

While Allan moved around the chair, shooting me from different angles, I got more and more depressed. It had been a nice dream, but it was now clear to me that I wasn't cut out to be a model. Not even close. I bit down on my back teeth to stop the tingling in my eyes that always meant tears were coming. To cry now would be the final and most awful embarrassment. I was determined not to do it.

"Done," he announced finally.

Springing from the chair, I grabbed my jacket and sprinted for the front door. Handsome Jim Corcoran looked at me as if I were nuts as I brushed past him and clattered down the steps.

I pushed my way out of the front door, and the cold wind slapped my wet face. Outside, it was gray and the street was deserted. I'd have to catch a cab back up to the Calico agency to meet Eve.

Stepping out into the street, I raised my hand to wave down a cab as I'd seen Ashley do. It was beginning to grow dark, and the streetlights around me were blurred by the tears in my eyes. What an idiot I'd been ever to dream I could be a model!

Chapter Seven

———◆———

Oh, I'm sure it wasn't as bad as all that," Martin said kindly that night at dinner as I sat glumly making fork tracks in my instant mashed potatoes. I'd just finished telling Martin and Todd about my disastrous first—and probably last—day as a model. Eve had heard it in the car, and Mom was still taking her exam.

"Believe me, it was bad," I assured him.

"Look at the bright side," said Todd. "You must have set a new world record for having the shortest modeling career in history. Maybe *The Guinness Book of World Records* would be interested. You could send them one of your new photos to put beside the story."

"Todd, your sister feels bad enough," Martin scolded him gently.

"I wasn't trying to make her feel bad," Todd defended himself. "I think it would be cool to be in the *Book of*

World Records. That would be much more exciting than being a model."

I let out a sour laugh. "I'd probably be right next to a calf with two heads or a boy who sat in grape juice for a week."

"Wouldn't that be great?" cried Todd. He meant it, too! Weird as he was, I appreciated his trying to cheer me up.

"I don't see what the big deal is," said Eve. "Modeling is about the most superficial thing a person can do. It's not like you just blew your chance to win the Nobel Peace Prize or something like that. And it's not like it was your life's dream. It was a lark and it didn't pan out. So, I mean, who cares, really?"

"I care," I snapped at her.

"Eve, it was important to Nikki," Martin said. "You could be a little more sympathetic."

Eve looked at him angrily. "Oh, sure, whatever Nikki does is important. I forgot."

Martin sighed. "Eve, I simply meant that as a family, when one member suffers a disappointment, we all—"

He was cut short by the sound of the phone ringing. I reached back to grab it. "Hello?"

"Hello, this is Renata Marco. May I speak to Nicole?"

I went pale. Had the photographer already told the agency how awful I was? "This is Nicole," I said in a shaky voice. "Hi."

"Hi," said Renata. "I'm calling to set up an appointment for you to go over your photos with Ms. Calico."

I swallowed hard. "She's seen them already?"

"Yes, Allan developed them right away and sent them over by messenger. Can you come in tomorrow at four?"

"One second, please," I said. Covering the phone with my hand, I looked over at Eve. "Can you take me in tomorrow after school?"

"I guess so, if you pay for gas."

"Yes, I can make it," I told Renata. "Is there something wrong with the pictures?"

"I don't know. Kate just asked me to call you," Renata replied. "They're probably fine."

"All right. Thanks for calling," I said, hanging up the phone.

"See?" said Martin cheerfully. "They didn't fire you. They want to see you tomorrow!"

"Yeah, so Ms. Calico can fire me in person," I said.

After I helped load the dishwasher, I went upstairs to do some homework. I wondered if I could get my old class schedule back now that I was no longer a model. It seemed awfully unfair that when this was over, all I'd have to show for it was having Mr. Eagleton for math.

I stared down at the book but couldn't pay attention. So I went downstairs and brought the cordless phone back to my room to call Dee.

"Hi!" she said. "How was it today? Tell me everything!"

"It was terrible," I told her. "I'm pretty sure they're going to fire me."

"No! Really?" she said. "I bet you were better than you thought."

"I didn't know what I was doing," I said, the words catching in my throat. "I was stiff and I wasn't smiling right."

"How can you smile wrong?" Dee asked.

"I don't know, but I did. I was supposed to smile with my eyes."

"What does that mean?"

"Who knows?" I cried. "I didn't have the slightest idea what to do. I wasn't dressed right. I didn't have the right makeup. I didn't know how to pose."

"Well, it was just your first time," Dee sympathized.

"It was my last time, too. Ms. Calico wants to see me tomorrow."

"Is that like being called to the principal's office?" Dee asked.

"I think so."

"Oh," said Dee sadly. "Well, um…look at the bright side. If they fire you, you'll have more time to work on the Oktoberfest Dance. The meeting was awesome. Kathy and I signed up for the decorating committee. We signed you up for it, too."

"Thanks," I said. "Oh, guess who I saw today? Mark!"

"Who?"

"The guy on my poster. You know, the surfer."

"Super cool!" Dee squealed. "Was he as gorgeous in real life?"

"Even better," I told her, glancing at the poster. "His real name is Jim. I guess I won't be able to call him Mark anymore."

"Wouldn't it be wild if you got to know him and went out with him and married him and everything?" Dee said. "It would be like you were psychic when you picked out that poster."

"That's a nice idea," I said. "But I don't think I'll ever see him again after today. Sorry, I know how much you wanted that limo ride."

"It's okay. I'll live," she said. "There are just three and a half years until the prom. I'll make sure I go with someone who hires a limo. I'll save up and hire it myself if I have to." One thing I love about Dee is that she always says the right thing.

Dee and I talked about the dance a little more and then hung up. I lay back on my bed and looked up at my poster of Jim. I thought about Ashley and Chloe. What exciting lives they had. I sighed sadly, thinking of all the wonderful things that I'd never experience now that I was no longer going to be a model.

Chapter Eight

———◆———

The next day, Eve dropped me off at the agency. When I stepped off the elevator, the reception area was filled with more hopefuls. "Ms. Calico said for me to send you right in," said Evelyn, the receptionist. The model hopefuls looked at me enviously. If they'd only known why I was going to see Ms. Calico, they would have been happy. There would soon be room for one new girl to take my place.

"Hello, dear, I'm glad you could come," Ms. Calico said when I came into her office. She took a manila folder off her desk and went to her silky, colorfully striped couch. "Come sit," she said, patting the cushion beside her.

Suddenly something inside me felt as if it were crumbling. I couldn't move from the spot where I stood. Like a fool, I started to cry. Not big sobs or anything, but tears were unmistakably leaking out of the corners of my eyes. "What is it, Nikki? What's wrong?" asked Ms. Calico, holding her hands out in concern.

That made me cry harder. "I'm really sorry," I said, jamming my palms into my eyes and sniffling. "I didn't mean to do this."

"Nonsense. Come sit," she said. She got up and put her arm around my quivering shoulders. Gently she guided me to the couch.

"If you'd give me another chance, I could do better. I know I could. It was just my first time, and I didn't know. I didn't even know to wear any makeup, but now I do, and I'll learn to smile with my eyes, whatever that means. I'll practice and—"

"Shh! Stop," said Ms. Calico. "I'm not going to let you go."

"You're not?"

"No."

"Then why did you want to see me?"

Ms. Calico smiled. "For two reasons. First, I wanted to go over these photos with you. I do that with every new model after the first shoot." She pulled one of several sheets of photos out of the folder. The photos were each about one inch square, and they were in rows. "These are called proofs," she explained. "From these proofs, you pick two or three photos that you like, and Allan Morgan will enlarge them for you to put into your portfolio. Then you will go to several other photographers for more photos. After you begin to work professionally, you'll add those pictures from ads you appear in, until you have a very impressive portfolio."

Peeking over, I saw the photos she held, and I cringed. I looked stiffer than a dummy in a department store.

"Yes, I agree," Ms. Calico said, looking at my expression. "These photos are not a success. We see nothing here of the inner Nicole. I see only a very pretty, but very frightened girl. In a real ad campaign there would be nothing here that could be used."

"How do I stop looking terrified?" I asked.

"By using your mind," she replied. "Many people think modeling is a mindless profession, but they're wrong. It takes imagination and discipline."

"Imagination?"

"Very much so. You must learn to think of the camera in one of two ways. Either you must forget it completely or you must pretend it is someone you are relating to in a certain way. Is it a parent you want to impress or a boy you want to flirt with? Is it the sun warming you? The important thing is that you have a story going on in your mind that lends interest to the picture."

"What does smiling with your eyes mean?" I asked.

"See this photo." She pointed to a photo on the sheet. "Technically you are smiling here. The corners of your mouth are up, but your face doesn't look happy. Your eyes are filled with anxiety. Smiling with your eyes means that your happiness is coming from within. It's expressed in your eyes and your entire face."

"But what if you don't feel happy?"

"What if an actress doesn't feel happy when she goes onstage to play a happy scene?" Ms. Calico countered.

"I guess she uses her imagination and pretends," I answered.

"Exactly."

Ms. Calico slipped a large photograph from the folder. "Here is the photo for your portfolio," she said. "Allan Morgan enlarged it without even asking."

I looked down at the picture she was holding. It was the candid shot Allan had taken while I was gathering my clothing and looking at Jim Corcoran. I had to admit, it was a beautiful picture. Golden light was streaming in through the window. It shone on my hair and one side of my face. The clothing I was holding draped gracefully from my arms, and my face had an excited expression.

"I don't know what you were looking at, but I can tell it interested and pleased you," Ms. Calico continued. "It's all there in your face—surprise, longing, excitement. You have a wonderfully expressive face. If you can produce just one picture like this every time you work, you will be a star."

This was the last thing I'd expected to hear. I was dumbstruck—but happy and relieved.

"Now there's a smile." Ms. Calico laughed, clapping her hands in delight. "That's the smile the world must see."

"So this means I can still be a model," I said foolishly.

"Yes, of course. Which brings me to the second thing I want to discuss with you. I'm working on a very big assignment with the ad agency for Cotton Kids."

"My mom always bought their stuff when I was little," I recalled. "They had those great pajamas with the trap-door bottoms."

"That's right. They're known for their children's clothing, but they're expanding their line to teen items. The company is investing a lot of money in a huge ad campaign to promote this new line. They've asked me to assemble some preteen and teen models for them to choose from. I'd like you to come in this Saturday and interview for the ad campaign. If you're selected, it will be great experience, good exposure, and you'll get to go to Bermuda for the shoot."

"Bermuda!" I said excitedly. I'd never been anywhere more exotic than the New Jersey shore.

"Yes. They want to introduce a line of summer wear, and they felt Bermuda would be a good spot to show it off. During that shoot, they'll select a boy and a girl to be the spokespersons for the new line, which will mean a lot of guaranteed bookings. Right now they're leaning toward Jim Corcoran for the boy, but the girl's slot is still wide open."

Jim Corcoran, in Bermuda! What could be better?

I *had* to get this job! "I'll be here," I said. "What should I wear? What time?"

"Nine-thirty. Wear something sporty. No, on second thought, come in at nine. Franz will be here doing some of the girls' hair. I think your hair could use some kind of lift. Maybe a new cut. Let him look at it."

"Sure," I agreed. As I got up from the couch, I felt a tremendous urge to hug Ms. Calico, but I didn't think that would be appropriate. So I just smiled one more time and left her office.

The minute I got out into the hall, I ran into Ashley. "Hi," she chirped. She looked great, as ever, in a flared red plaid jumper, with olive green leggings and red ballet shoes. Her hair was pulled up in a high ponytail.

"Hi," I replied, still feeling shaken from my interview with Ms. Calico.

"You look kind of dazed," Ashley noted. "Is anything wrong?"

"I just came from a meeting with Ms. Calico," I told her. "I did so badly at my photo shoot yesterday that I thought she was going to dump me, for sure. But one picture came out really well so it was all right."

"It must be hard at first," Ashley sympathized. "Nobody really gives you any formal training. You just have to pick it up as you go along."

"Does everyone go through this?"

"Go through what?"

"Feeling like they don't have what it takes to be a model," I said.

"Is that how you feel?" Ashley asked.

"Yes," I admitted. Before I could say more, she took hold of my arm and began leading me along. "Where are we going?" I asked.

"The hallway is no place to have a serious talk," she

said. "I know somewhere we can have some privacy."

We turned a corner and went down a quiet, empty hall. At the end of the hall was a closed door. "Make sure no one is coming," Ashley said. Then, with a quick peek over her shoulder, she slipped inside and pulled me with her.

She flipped a switch and an eerie red glow lit the room. Inside were two industrial sinks and a lot of strange-looking equipment. On the wall was a large framed poster of a young woman wearing white boots and a minidress. Her dark hair fell to her waist, and her bangs were thick and long. She wore tons of bracelets and big ball earrings. Her lipstick was white.

"Guess who that is?" said Ashley.

I went up to the poster and stared at it. The woman was beautiful and she looked familiar, but I couldn't place her.

"Kate Calico!" Ashley giggled.

It was! I could hardly believe it. "What is this room?" I asked.

"It belongs to Kate's husband, Maurice. He does some of his photography work in here. He says the red light makes him feel more creative." She rolled her eyes. "He's kind of weird. Anyway, I named this the Red Room."

"Ms. Calico's husband is a photographer?" I asked.

"He's a photographer and filmmaker," Ashley explained. "He launched Kate's career when he took that picture of her as a teenager."

"Have you ever met him?" I asked.

Ashley shook her head. "No, but Renata told me that his films are really strange."

"Wow," I said, impressed. "Are we allowed to be in here?"

"Probably not. This is our secret place—mine and Chloe's. We come here when we're upset or stressed out, or if we're between appointments and we need a quiet place to do homework."

"How did you find it?"

"I was dying to find out what was in this room, so one day I just slipped in when no one was around. The door's never locked."

Ashley sat cross-legged on the floor. "So tell me all about how you've been feeling. You don't still think you're about to be dumped, do you?"

"No," I said. "Ms. Calico told me to come in Saturday and try out for a shoot."

"Cotton Kids, right?" Ashley guessed. "I'm coming in for that, too. It would be so cool to go to Bermuda together. We'd have a blast!"

"I would love to get that job," I said.

"Don't worry. You'll be fine. I can tell," Ashley said kindly. "I've been in this business a long time. I've seen lots of girls come and go. Some have what it takes, some don't. But you do."

"I hope so," I said, perching on the corner of a table. "But how can you be so sure? I can't imagine you ever feeling insecure."

Ashley hooted disdainfully.

"What's so funny?"

"Me, not insecure! That's a laugh. I'm insecure all the time. I'm the queen of insecurity."

"You're so pretty and successful. What do you have to be insecure about?" I asked.

"You try being the daughter of Taylor Andrews and the sister of John Renee," Ashley said.

"John Renee is your brother?" I cried. John Renee was only one of the best-looking television stars around. Right now he was in a show about young telephone repairmen who live together in this big house. It was called "One Ashford Avenue." I made sure to watch it every week.

"He's my half brother," Ashley said. "If I go out with my mother, we're mobbed by people wanting her autograph. If John is with us, they want his autograph, too. Then they see me and wrinkle their noses like, 'Who the heck is she?' Or someone might say, 'Didn't I see you in some spaghetti ad?' It makes me feel like a big nobody."

"But you feel like a nobody only because you're with such super somebodies. If you were just a regular person like me, being a model would make you a big shot."

"A regular person," Ashley echoed. "That sounds so great. A lot of times I wish I were just a regular person. But I never can be because of my family. I envy you. I bet you have a normal mom and dad and some brothers and sisters."

"Well, I have a stepdad, Martin, who's great. And I have a pesty little brother. It's my stepsister, Eve, who is the pain. All my life I wished for a big sister. But I ended up with the big sister from Mars!"

Ashley laughed. "Is she that bad? Really?"

"Worse," I said, but I had to laugh, too. "I think she's jealous that Martin and I get along so well. She and Martin always seem to fight. Eve is so grumpy—she argues with everyone. Maybe she's so smart that other people seem stupid to her."

"My brother and I get along great, but I don't see him too often. He lives out in California, near my dad."

"Your parents are divorced?" I asked delicately.

"Yeah. I have a stepfather, too. He's an assistant movie director, so he travels a lot. He's okay, but we're not very close."

Just then the doorknob turned and Chloe walked in. She stopped in her tracks the minute she saw us. "What is *she* doing here?" she asked Ashley.

"We were only talking," Ashley answered.

"This is our secret place!" Chloe said indignantly.

"I didn't think you'd mind," Ashley said. "Nikki is so great. I know you'll like her once—"

"That's not the point!" said Chloe. "This is *our* place. You should have asked me."

"I'm sorry, Chloe, but you shouldn't be so—"

"Don't you tell me how I should be," Chloe snapped in an angry whisper. "You don't even know me these days!"

Chapter Nine

———— ◆ ————

This dance will take a total commitment from all of you, but I'm sure it will be a great success," said Mrs. Laskin as the Oktoberfest Dance meeting broke up that Friday afternoon. "I'll expect those finance reports by next week."

Caitlin Thomas, who was heading up the decorating committee, came over to Dee, Kathy, and me. "The committee members are going out for burgers tomorrow so we can discuss who is going to do what. We'll meet at the Burger Bar down the street at noon. Okay?"

"Okay!" Dee said excitedly. "We'll be there."

"This is so great," said Kathy when Caitlin was gone. "It's turning out just the way I'd hoped."

"I can't go," I said in a quiet voice.

"Why not?" Dee cried. "This is the first real planning meeting. You want to get a good assignment, don't you?"

"I have a tryout for a big modeling job," I told them. "If I'm picked, I'll get to go to Bermuda."

"Excuse us!" said Kathy. "I guess a dance seems pretty dull compared to a modeling job in Bermuda."

"It's not that," I argued. "I just have to be there. If I don't show up for jobs, they'll stop asking me to come in."

"This modeling thing is taking up more time than I thought," Dee grumbled.

"What did you expect?" I asked.

"I don't know," Dee sulked. "I figured it was something you'd do when you weren't with us. I didn't think it would take up so much of your time. We never see you anymore."

"That's not true," I protested.

"It is true," Kathy said. "We're not in the same classes anymore, and we only see you for half a lunch period. Sometimes! And when you are around, you're trying to cram in your schoolwork."

"If I start failing, my parents will say I can't model!" I defended myself. "What do you guys want from me?"

"Sorry," Dee said. "I suppose we're just being selfish. We miss you, you know."

"I miss you, too," I said. "Things will get better once I get some kind of modeling schedule."

"They'll probably only get worse as you get busier," Kathy said glumly.

I sighed deeply. What could I say? It wasn't as if I didn't want to do things with them. I did! It was just that my life had suddenly become incredibly busy.

"It's all right," Dee said. "We'll work it out. Why don't we all go to the movies Sunday afternoon?"

"I can't," I said, feeling terrible. "I have a ton of homework and a history paper. Sunday is the only day I have to do it."

"Oh, well," said Dee with a shrug. "I guess we just don't fit into your schedule anymore."

I went home feeling pretty crummy. My friends were slipping away from me, and I didn't know what to do about it.

Saturday morning Eve dropped me off at the agency just before nine. "I'm supposed to see Franz about my hair," I told Evelyn. She sent me back to where a handsome guy in a tight red T-shirt was doing the hair of Brittany Wells, a tall black girl of about sixteen with a long mass of thick dark curls. Her face was on practically every teen magazine cover imaginable. Even though she was young, she was a real superstar.

Franz was pulling her long hair into a French braid. He didn't seem to notice me as I entered, but without turning, he said, "Have a seat, Red. I'll be right there."

I'd been waiting only a few minutes when Tracey Morris walked in. She was wearing her usual dark glasses. With a flare of pink, she blew a gum bubble and let it pop. "Hi," I said, glad to see a familiar face.

"Hi," she replied with a quick smile. "Are you here to be made over, too?"

"Well, Ms. Calico said she wanted Franz to look at my hair before the Cotton Kids interview."

"I don't know if I want anyone messing with my hair," Tracey grumbled, fingering the ends of her shoulder-length dark hair.

"It's a free haircut," I said, remembering how Tracey had been so concerned with the money when we won the contest.

"Yeah, I guess." Tracey took a seat beside me, stretching out her long legs. "So how are you doing with this modeling thing?"

"It's a little strange," I admitted. "I'm not so sure I'm too good at it, for one thing."

Tracey laughed. "You, too? My first test shoot was the pits. The photographer kept telling me I didn't look joyous enough. How the heck am I supposed to be joyous with bright lights glaring in my eyes?"

I found myself smiling, happy to hear I wasn't the only one who had started out badly. "Did you want to die?" I asked.

"No, I wanted to punch out the photographer," Tracey replied. "He really bugged me." She sighed. "Maybe it's me. Everyone's been bugging me lately."

"Why?" I asked.

"I don't know. It's like my friends have developed this attitude since I became a model. They don't understand that I'm busy, and they think I think I'm hot stuff. But I haven't changed. It's all in their heads."

"I know exactly what you mean," I said. "They seem to think you don't want to be bothered with them anymore."

"Yeah," Tracey agreed. "They're so sensitive. I feel I have to keep proving that I want to be their friend, but I have less time than ever before. It's a real drag."

"Tell me about it!" I said. "I don't want to lose my friends, though."

"I know how you feel," Tracey said seriously. "But friends or not, I'm sticking with this. I got my first thousand-dollar check, and it sure felt good. My mom has been supporting us on her own for years, and we barely squeak by. Now I can help her."

Franz finished Brittany's hair and then looked at me. "Okay, Red, your turn." I went to the chair where Brittany had sat. Franz squinted at me as he tapped his chin thoughtfully. "Curls might be nice, but I don't think your hair would take them well. Any objection to having me cut layers?"

"No," I said.

"All right. That's what we'll do. It will give your hair body."

I was sort of nervous as Franz began spritzing my hair with water and snipping it. When he was done, though, I loved the way I looked. I shook my head, and my hair seemed to bounce from shoulder to shoulder.

"The layers make your eyes look enormous," Franz commented. "It's just what you needed." He turned to Tracey. "You next, Shades."

Tracey peeled off her glasses, revealing her startling aqua eyes. "Oh!" Franz exclaimed. "Those eyes will make you a star, honey. Let's get that ratty hair off your face and highlight them."

I stepped out into the hall, and the moment I did, Ms. Calico seemed to swoop down on me from out of nowhere. "Your hair looks lovely," she said as she took my wrist. "Come with me and do just as I say."

She pulled me into a room with a long table. Sitting at the end of the table were two men in suits and a woman, also in a gray tailored suit. "Take off your shoes, Nikki," said Ms. Calico.

I looked at her questioningly. "Just do it," she said. "Socks, too."

Slipping off my shoes and socks, I felt the deep plush carpeting under my feet. "Now I want you to leap up onto that table as if it were a balance beam," she instructed me. "Show us a balance beam routine."

It was totally crazy, but what else could I do? Usually I used a springboard to get up onto the beam. Since there was none around, I stepped on a chair and then onto the table. Lifting one leg back and leaning forward, I did an arabesque; then I went into a forward roll. It was hard to roll on the table because I only had one edge to grip, but of course there was a wider surface and less risk of falling.

I came out of the roll and kicked my legs forward. By then I was at the end of the table. "I'll need you to move so I can dismount," I told the men and woman.

They stepped aside and I did a cartwheel off the edge of the table. "Bravo!" Ms. Calico cried, applauding. "Didn't I tell you she was wonderful? Imagine the photo opportunities with a girl who can do these things. What better way to promote the sturdiness and stretchability of the Cotton Kids teen line?"

"We know she looks good in a bathing suit from the photo you showed us," said the woman. "And she is lovely."

It was weird being spoken about as if I weren't there.

"I say she's a definite," said one of the men.

"I agree, J.B.," said the other man. "She has that wholesome look we want. All-American."

Ms. Calico smiled at me triumphantly. "You did it, Nikki. Start packing for Bermuda!"

Chapter Ten

es, the more I think about it, the more I'm sure," said Tracey as we waited outside the Calico Modeling Agency for Eve. "This is the coolest thing that has ever happened to me."

"Becoming a model?" I asked as a cold wind blew my new, bouncy hair around. The day had turned rainy, and the chilly air made me shiver.

"No, getting to go to Bermuda," Tracey answered. With her new haircut, she now looked like a model to me. Franz had trimmed her hair up to her chin at a steep angle. It was very fashionable and it made her eyes look huge.

"I just hope I can go," I said.

"What do you mean?" asked Tracey.

"My parents are so protective. I can't imagine them letting me go off to Bermuda."

"You can bring a chaperone," Tracey reminded me.

"Mom has law school Friday nights and Saturday afternoons, and Martin works weekends a lot. I doubt they'll be able to get away."

"That's tough," Tracey said sympathetically. "My mother is already psyched. She said she'd get the time off, no matter what. There's no way she'd pass up a free trip to Bermuda."

"I wish my parents felt more like your mother," I said.

"My mother loves traveling. She backpacked her way through Europe after college, and when she and my father were still together, they drove across the country and lived in their car."

"Wow!" I said, impressed. "That sounds so cool."

Tracey checked her watch. "Are you sure your sister won't mind taking me home?"

"She'll mind, because Eve minds everything. But you live only ten minutes away. I don't see why you should take the train. If she grouches, just ignore her." As I was speaking, Eve's car swung around the corner, wheels squealing. She screeched up to the curb and we got in.

"This is Tracey," I told Eve. "She lives over at the Paradise Gardens Apartments."

"What do I look like, a limo service?" Eve barked.

"I'll take the train," said Tracey, already getting out of the car.

Eve squinted at Tracey. "Don't I know you?"

Tracey studied Eve for a moment. "Were you in the Gifted and Talented program over at the college?" she asked at last.

Eve's face broke into a rare smile. "Yes! I remember you now. You were in the beginning engineering course."

"Eve Myers!" Tracey cried. "Sure, I remember. You told the class you want to work for NASA."

"Right! And, let me think…. You were interested in expansion bridge engineering."

"That's right. I think it's so fascinating."

I couldn't believe my ears. When Tracey had written that stuff on her contest card about being gifted and talented, I'd assumed she was just goofing. But apparently she was for real. She was as big a brain as Eve!

"I don't mind driving you," said Eve. "Come on."

"Thanks," Tracey said, settling into the backseat. "Hey, I have an idea, Nikki! What if Eve went with you to Bermuda?"

I caught my breath, speechless. I couldn't think of a better way to ruin a wonderful time.

"No way," Eve said quickly. "There's not a chance I'd hang around with a bunch of fluffhead models or their boring old parents. Count me out."

"But you could spend all day at the beach," Tracey said, trying to persuade her.

"I hate sand," said Eve sourly.

I made a face at Eve and looked back at Tracey. "I think Mom would want a *real* adult to be with me," I said, "not some overgrown kid."

"Watch it," Eve warned under her breath.

We drove for about twenty minutes. Tracey and Eve talked about their engineering course the whole time. As we neared home, Tracey suddenly leaned forward to the front seat. "I've got it! We'll introduce my mother to your mother and convince her that my mother can chaperone the two of us."

"You *are* a genius!" I exclaimed. "That's a great idea. Let's do it right now. Is your mother home?"

"I think so," Tracey said.

"Eve, my mom is home, too. Can we swing by the house, pick her up, and bring her to Tracey's house?"

"Give me a break," Eve replied. But she glanced up to her rearview mirror and looked at Tracey. "Oh, all right," she said, giving in.

As soon as we were parked in the driveway, I jumped out of the car. "Come on, Tracey," I said. "You can call your mother from inside." We ran into the house and found Mom vacuuming. "Use the phone in the kitchen," I shouted to Tracey over the vacuum's roar.

"Mom, you have to come with me," I yelled, pulling the machine's plug from the wall.

"What? Where?" she asked.

I ran to the coat closet and pulled out her corduroy jacket. "You'll see. Just come on."

"How did your interview go?"

"Great! I got picked."

Mom clapped her hands together in delight. "That's wonderful."

"It means I'll get to go to Bermuda," I said.

The smile slipped from Mom's face. "For how long?"

"Three days. Friday to Sunday."

"When?"

"The weekend after next."

Mom folded her arms and sighed. "Nikki, this is so sudden. I can't get away and I don't think Martin—"

"Don't worry, Mom. I have it all figured out."

"My mother says it's fine with her," said Tracey, coming out of the kitchen.

"This is Tracey Morris, Mom," I said. "Her mother says it's okay, so let's go."

Mom shook her head and laughed nervously. "What's going on? What's okay? I feel like I'm being hijacked."

"You are." I laughed. "You always tell me to be open-minded, so now it's your turn."

"All right," Mom agreed, allowing me to drag her out the door and into the car.

After a ten-minute ride, Eve pulled into the parking lot of the Paradise Gardens Apartments. "I'll wait in the car," she said.

Mom looked around. "Would you please tell me what is going on?"

"This way," Tracey said as she led us from the car into a courtyard. In the center was an empty, mossy pool. The apartment building was covered with siding that was the same dull aqua as the pool.

The three-story apartment complex looked as if it might have been nice at one time, but now it was run-down. The courtyard lawn was scrubby and full of weeds. And the fact that the sky chose that moment to drizzle just added to the overall dreariness.

I sneaked a quick look at Mom. She was wearing her serious, what's-going-on face. I've seen it before. Her eyes move all around in small, quick movements, like she's taking snapshots of everything to load into her brain. It's amazing how much she notices.

We walked up one flight of stairs to the second floor. Tracey led us to her door and opened it with her key. "Mom!" she shouted as she pushed open the door.

The apartment was incredibly messy. The chairs were draped with clothing, and a table was almost buried under the books, magazines, papers, and mail on top of it.

"Mom!" Tracey yelled again. From out of the kitchen came a slim woman with frizzy blond hair. She wore jeans and a tie-dyed sweatshirt but no shoes. "Hi, there," she greeted us, her voice soft and girlish. "I'm Caroline Morris. You'll have to excuse the mess. I'm not the best of housekeepers, but the place doesn't usually look this bad. The minute Tracey called and said she had been picked, I pulled out all my summer things. Isn't this exciting? I've always wanted to go to Bermuda!"

"It is exciting," Mom agreed cautiously. "I'm sorry I can't get away to go with Nikki."

"Oh, yes, it is a shame. But Tracey told me the plan and I wouldn't mind looking after Nikki, not one bit," said Mrs. Morris, smiling at me. She seemed the exact opposite of Tracey, all bubbly and full of enthusiasm.

"Tracey!" she cried happily. "Look at that haircut! You look so cute."

"Thanks," Tracey mumbled.

"I've made us some herbal tea," Mrs. Morris told Mom. "Let's discuss this trip."

Mom followed her into a small kitchen, which was cluttered with dishes. Mrs. Morris pushed aside a pile of newspapers in order to make room on the table. "This recycling thing catches up with me," she said. "It makes housekeeping even harder, but we all have to do our part."

I was afraid Mrs. Morris might be too much of a hippie type for Mom. She might worry that Mrs. Morris wouldn't be strict enough. And the messiness wasn't a good sign, either. Mom always says an orderly space reflects an orderly mind. I didn't think she was going to be too impressed with the orderliness of Mrs. Morris's mind.

"Want to hang out in my room?" Tracey offered.

"Sure," I said. We walked through the kitchen and down a long hall into a small bedroom. It was tidy, completely different from the whirlwind in the rest of the apartment. Three shelves crammed with books hung above a neat desk. On the wall was a big black-and-white poster of Albert Einstein. Next to Einstein was another poster of a guy on a motorcycle. "Who's he?" I asked.

Tracey shrugged. "I just liked the bike."

"Oh, come on," I scoffed.

Tracey smiled. "All right. I did think the guy was pretty cute, too. I don't know who he is."

"You won't believe this, but I have a poster of a guy I don't know on my wall, too," I admitted. "Only it turns out he's Jim Corcoran."

"Jim Corcoran?" Tracey mused. "He was there when they were interviewing my group. I'm pretty sure they picked him."

I held up two sets of crossed fingers. "I have to go on this trip. I *have* to."

"Let's see how they're doing," Tracey suggested.

My fists clenched tight with nervousness, I opened Tracey's door. Together we stepped quietly into the hall.

I heard my mother laugh loudly. "Yes, yes, I remember that," she said happily. "And wasn't it amazing when Dylan sang 'The Times They Are A-Changin' ' at that peace rally in Boston? I was covered with goosebumps."

I looked at Tracey in complete astonishment. My mother had been at a peace rally in Boston?

Then Mrs. Morris did a raspy imitation of Bob Dylan singing, and Mom exploded with laughter once again.

This was too weird for me! I never expected my mom and Mrs. Morris to get along so well. But I thought it was a good sign. Bermuda suddenly seemed so close that I could almost smell the suntan lotion.

Chapter Eleven

Earth to Nikki, come in." As if from very far away, I heard Dee's voice. "Ooohhh, Nicole."

"Sorry," I said, snapping back to reality. I had been in the middle of a daydream. I was imagining Jim Corcoran and myself jogging together on a Bermuda beach.

"Caitlin asked if you'd be free to help set up chairs and tables the night before the dance," said Kathy.

We were sitting in a classroom on Tuesday after school with the eight other members of the decorating committee. All eyes were on me. "What's the date of the dance, again?" I asked, completely embarrassed that I couldn't remember.

"October fifth," said Caitlin Thomas, rolling her eyes. "The first weekend in October, remember?"

My hand flew to my mouth. Somehow I had never put

it together. I knew my flight for the Cotton Kids shoot would be the weekend after next. And I knew the dance was the first weekend of October. But it had never occurred to me that they would overlap. Time was flying by so quickly!

"What's the matter?" Dee asked.

I took a deep breath. How could I tell them my problem now? Here, in front of everyone?

"Uh, no, I can't do it that night," I said in a small voice.

"Everyone else has volunteered," said Caitlin, obviously annoyed.

"Well, I, uh, I have to work that night."

"She's a model," Dee filled in for me.

With another roll of her eyes, Caitlin crossed my name off her list. "All right, everyone," she said. "We'll see you all—except Nikki—on Friday. Don't forget to bring your staplers and glue guns. Kathy, Dee, and Nikki, did you get all the autumn leaves cut out?"

"Yes, absolutely," Kathy spoke up. "We'll be sure to bring them."

As the group got up and went their separate ways, Kathy grabbed my arm and pulled me out into the hall, with Dee close behind. "What do you mean, you have to work Friday? How could you take a job the night before the dance?"

"I didn't have any choice," I told her.

"I can't believe you forgot the date of the dance," Dee said. "Your head is really in the clouds."

"Listen, I lied in there," said Kathy. "We don't have nearly enough fall leaves. Both of you come over tonight and we'll cut some more." She looked at me with narrowed eyes. "If we'd had *everyone's* full cooperation, we'd be all right. But as you know, we were shorthanded some afternoons. You *can* come tonight, can't you, Nikki?"

"I'll come tonight, but I do have a problem," I said slowly. "A big problem."

"What's that?" asked Dee.

"I can't go to the dance."

"What?" Kathy shrieked.

"Remember my big Bermuda job? Well, it's the same weekend."

Kathy swung her body away from me and shouted to the walls, "This is unbelievable! Didn't you realize this before?"

"I spent all of Sunday worrying whether I'd be allowed to go. Ever since my parents finally said yes, I've been in sort of a trance. I guess my head just hasn't been on straight."

"No kidding," Dee quipped. "As if we hadn't noticed."

"I'm going to ask you something," said Kathy. The look in her eyes worried me. She was so angry. "Is modeling suddenly more important than us?"

"Of course not!" I blurted out desperately. It was true. I loved them both. I was simply doing the best I could to juggle two different worlds.

"Then how could you forget about this dance? We've

been planning it and talking about going for weeks," she went on.

"I know," I said. "But there was no way I could have predicted everything that's happened."

"Don't bother coming over tonight," Kathy grumbled. "Why should you help if you're not going to the dance, anyway."

"But I want to help," I insisted.

"No you don't," she said as she started to walk away from me. "You want to be a famous model."

Barely knowing which way to turn, Dee waved to me while she hurried down the hall to catch up with Kathy. I didn't blame her. All this time Kathy had been there for her. I hadn't. I'd either been at the Calico agency or trying to cram in schoolwork.

That afternoon Martin picked me up from school. "Why the long face?" he asked as soon as I got into the car.

"I forgot that the big Oktoberfest Dance is the same weekend as my modeling trip. Kathy and Dee are real mad at me."

"You could skip the trip," he said as we pulled away from the school.

"No I couldn't," I disagreed. "This is a big job. It's important to my modeling career."

"More important than your friends?" Martin asked.

"Why does it have to be a choice?" I replied. "Why can't I have both?"

"I know what you're going through," he said.

"You do?" I was doubtful. How could he?

"When I went away to college, some of the guys I hung out with in my old neighborhood didn't like it. They said I thought I was too good for them, and they didn't want to hang out with me anymore. They felt as if I'd deserted them."

"But you hadn't," I said. "You just wanted something for yourself. Did you lose all your friends?"

"No, not all," Martin said. "It takes work, though. You have to be there if you want to keep your friends. It's not easy. You have to decide how important modeling is to you. You can see already that it will require sacrifice."

"You didn't let your friends stop you from going to college."

"No. I really wanted an education."

"I really want to model," I said firmly. And as soon as the words came out of my mouth, I knew they were true.

The following week was pretty strange. I was so excited about Bermuda that I couldn't think of anything else. At the same time, I felt terrible that Kathy and Dee were ignoring me. They didn't come to my locker in the morning the way they usually did. And I guess I was ignoring them, too, because I didn't go find them for the second half of lunch. I didn't want to risk being given the cold shoulder.

On the Thursday afternoon before my trip, I found a note stuck in my locker. *Have a good trip.* It was written in Dee's loopy handwriting. It made me feel a little better.

Finally Friday came. Tracey and her mom picked me up in a cab at seven in the morning. Mrs. Morris was already wearing sunglasses and a big straw hat. Tracey had on her trademark sunglasses, but other than that she didn't look very summery in jeans and a long-sleeved T-shirt. "I'm not going to freeze," she said in her usual gruff way.

When we got to the airport, we met Renata. She was standing with Ashley and Chloe. "Hi," Ashley greeted us. Chloe just nodded.

"Hi," I said. "Isn't this exciting?"

Tracey and her mother hurried off to check their bags. "Isn't that another one of the new girls?" Ashley asked me when Tracey was gone.

"Yes. Her name is Tracey Morris," I said. "She's nice."

"If you say so," said Ashley, taking my arm and steering me away from Chloe and Renata. "Renata looks after Chloe and me on these kinds of trips. Where's your mother?"

"Tracey's mother is my chaperone," I told her. I glanced around and saw Jim Corcoran standing with Rachel Wright, another teen model. She had short blond hair and must have been almost six feet tall.

"The guy of your dreams is chatting with the evil princess," Ashley whispered in my ear.

"Why do you call her that?" I asked.

"She's a real snob. But don't worry—they're just friends."

"I don't even know him," I said.

"But you'd like to. I can tell," said Ashley.

Suddenly I felt embarrassed. "Is it that obvious?"

"Just to me," said Ashley. "Remember, I can tell things about people."

I looked over at Renata and Chloe. "I see you and Chloe made up."

"Mostly," Ashley said. "Chloe can't stay mad at me long. We're best friends."

A photographer, makeup artist, hairdresser, and the three representatives from the ad agency for whom I'd performed on the table all arrived. So did the rest of the models and some parents. We got our seat assignments and boarded the plane. Tracey and her mom got seats together, but I ended up alone in a seat several rows down.

I was gazing out the window when I had the feeling someone was staring at me. I turned and saw Chloe looking from her ticket to me and frowning deeply. "I guess this is my seat," she said, sitting beside me.

"Good," I said, trying to be pleasant. I wasn't sure why she disliked me, but I didn't want her to. Maybe we could get to know each other better on this trip.

I gripped my seat as the plane took off. I was a little nervous, since I'd never flown before. It was the strangest feeling I'd ever experienced. My stomach seemed to lurch forward, and I turned away from the window when we lifted off the ground.

"That's so weird," I said to Chloe, who sat coolly paging through a fashion magazine, barely noticing the takeoff.

She looked up from the magazine as if she'd heard a sound but wasn't sure what it was. Then, without answering, she went back to her magazine.

My stomach jumped as the plane leveled. For a while, I busied myself watching all the information about what to do in case of an emergency, which was being shown on television screens in the aisles. "I wonder how long you could tread water if the plane went down over the ocean," I said when they got to the part about seat cushions being used for floating.

"I haven't the slightest idea," said Chloe, not looking up.

When the emergency information was over, I settled back and watched the clouds outside my window. The sun was shining on them and it was really beautiful. "Would you like to look out for a bit?" I offered Chloe.

"Cloud gazing isn't my idea of a thrill," she said.

"I just didn't want to hog the window seat all to myself," I said.

Chloe still didn't say anything. I was really getting annoyed with her. "Is there a reason why you're being so rude to me?" I asked bluntly.

"Excuse me?" she said coldly, putting down her magazine.

"What's your problem with me? I've never done anything to you. Why are you so snobby to me?"

"I think you know the answer to that," Chloe replied.

"I have no idea what you're talking about."

"I have a right to be mad when someone tries to steal my best friend."

"What?" I cried.

Chloe turned in her seat and faced me. "Ashley and I have been best friends since I started modeling. Nobody can come between us."

"Can't a person have more than one best friend?" I asked.

"Of course not," Chloe hissed. "Best means *best* —the one that is better than all the others. You can have several good friends, but only one is your best!"

"I suppose that's true," I admitted. Had I really been trying to steal Ashley from her? No, that was crazy. Ashley was the one who had been friendly to me. I liked Ashley, but I wasn't trying to steal her from anybody.

While I sat trying to make sense of everything Chloe had said, she got up and changed seats without even saying a word.

I took out *Jane Eyre,* a book I was supposed to read for English class. I'd just begun reading when I sensed someone staring at me. When I glanced up, I was looking into Jim Corcoran's blue eyes!

"Excuse me, is this seat empty?" he asked.

"Uh…um…" Turning around, I saw that Chloe had found another seat several rows back. "I guess it's free."

"Great," said Jim, sitting beside me. "I got assigned

next to some guy who fell asleep and started snoring in my ear."

"Oh, that's terrible." I laughed.

"Tell me about it." He smiled as he stuffed his carry-on bag under the seat. "Your name is Nikki, isn't it?"

I bit my lip happily. He knew my name! "Yep, I'm Nikki Wilton. How did you know?"

"I asked about you that day when I saw you in the studio. I'm Jim Corcoran. I heard you had some test shots taken that day. I guess that means you're new to all this."

"This is my first real modeling job," I confessed. "I'm pretty nervous."

"There's nothing to it," he said. "Stick with me and I'll tell you everything you need to know."

"Okay, thanks," I said. I was trying hard not to grin from ear to ear.

Chapter Twelve

———◆———

The minute we stepped out of the Bermuda airport, I knew I was in the most amazing place I'd ever seen.

How can I describe it? All the colors were *more*. The blue sky was incredibly blue. The green of the palm trees was the greenest green in the world.

Two minivans pulled up, and Renata directed us toward them. I was hoping to sit with Jim, but Mrs. Morris latched on to my arm and drew me into a van with her and Tracey. "Isn't this thrilling?" she said.

"Mom, chill, would you?" said Tracey, settling into the van beside me.

"Life is too short to chill," said Mrs. Morris pleasantly. I knew just how she felt. As the van drove us toward the Grotto Azura resort where we would be staying, I was almost glued to the van window, staring out at the yellow, blue, green, and pink pastel homes that dotted the hillsides. My heart was soaring with excitement. Bermuda had to be the most beautiful place in the world.

As we drove up the long driveway to the resort, the sun disappeared and we were suddenly in the middle of a downpour. "Just a sun shower," said the driver, a tall black man in a crisp white shirt and black shorts. He stopped the van under a canopy at the front of the resort's main building.

"Calico models, come with me," Renata said as we climbed out of the van. "We'll get our room assignments and then meet on the patio by the pool for lunch."

We got our keys and I hurried to the room I would be sharing with Tracey and her mother. Ripping off my jeans and sweatshirt, I pulled on a sundress and slipped into the new sandals I'd bought. "You look great," I said as Tracey zipped up a denim romper.

"Thanks," she said, almost shyly. "So long, Mom. We're headed to the patio for lunch."

"Have fun," her mother shouted from the bathroom.

Almost running, Tracey and I headed down toward the pool. The rain had stopped but it was still overcast. Beside the pool was a patio area under a large yellow tent. It was surrounded by a vine-covered trellis. From a distance I spotted Renata, dressed in a gauzy white caftan, her hair piled up on her head. She was sitting with the adults. The models were scattered at other tables.

When we arrived at the patio, Ashley was sitting at the

same table as Jim. So was Chloe. But I was determined not to be intimidated by Chloe's rudeness. "Come on, let's sit over there," I said, pulling Tracey along.

"Try this fruit platter. It's awesome," said Ashley as we sat down. In the center of the table was a platter loaded with all kinds of fruit.

Rachel Wright plucked a strawberry from the platter and dangled it in front of Jim. "Here, Jimmy, I've got something for you," she teased.

"Get out of here," he said, grabbing the strawberry and tossing it into the bushes. "You know I can't eat that!" He looked at me and explained, "I'm allergic to strawberries. It's not serious, but I get a rash if I eat them. It wouldn't be bad if I didn't happen to be a model. A rash doesn't exactly look great in a picture."

Rachel pretended to pout. "You're so fussy about what you eat, Jimmy. Every morning you have the same dull health shake, and everything else you eat is healthy, healthy, healthy. It's so boring."

"Yes, but look at that thick hair, that healthy complexion, those shining eyes," said Ashley. I couldn't tell if she was teasing or not. He *did* have all those things, after all. "In this profession it pays to be healthy," Ashley went on. "It pays off in real dollars, too. Jim is sure to be the Cotton Kids spokesguy."

"That's not set yet," Jim objected. "They're going to take some shots this afternoon and announce who the spokescouple is tomorrow."

Rachel draped her long arm along Jim's shoulder and smiled. It was clear she figured they made a cute couple and were the likely choice.

"I hope they pick me," Ashley sighed, plunking her chin into her hand. "I'd love a contract for commercials."

"Forget commercials," Chloe scoffed. "You're going to be in a movie soon."

"You are?" Rachel asked eagerly.

"*Maybe*," Ashley said. "Or maybe not. My brother is trying to get me into this TV movie they're making from his TV series. I probably won't even get a part."

The waiter came with everyone else's food—four salads. Tracey and I ordered burgers and fries. After lunch, Renata told us to be on the beach on the opposite side of the patio in an hour. "Keep your makeup to a minimum because you'll be in the hot sun, and don't forget your sunblock," she said. "Although it's still a little overcast, it's clearing up quickly. Even on an overcast day, the sun here is much stronger than at home. You'll burn much faster."

When Renata left, we all got up to go back to our rooms. Ashley started to walk along with Tracey and me when Chloe called to her, "Want to take a quick swim in the pool?"

"I can't," Ashley replied.

"You don't have to get your hair wet," Chloe pressed.

"It's not that," said Ashley. "You heard what Renata said on the plane. She checked my horoscope and it said to beware of nature today."

Chloe looked so disappointed that Ashley gave in. "I'll hang my feet over the side while you swim," she said. "But if I fall in the water and crack my head open, it will be your fault."

"That won't happen," said Chloe, ruffling her short black hair with her hands and looking happy once again.

Ashley went off with Chloe, and Tracey and I headed to our room. We were nearly there when I realized I was barefoot. "My new sandals!" I cried. I had kicked them off under the table and forgotten to put them back on. "I'm going to get them," I told Tracey. "I'll be right back."

I hurried along the path to the patio. Except for waiters clearing the last of the lunch dishes, the place was empty. Luckily my sandals were still under the table. I scooped them up and was about to leave when I spotted Jim Corcoran over by the trellis. His back was to me and he was leaning forward.

I wondered if he was sick and using the trellis for support. Concerned, I went over to see if I could help. Though I wasn't trying to sneak up on him, he didn't hear me coming. Through the vines, I could see there were chairs and tables with umbrellas on the other side of the trellis.

I froze as I realized what Jim was doing. He was trying to hear what someone on the other side was saying.

Now I was curious. I wanted to find out what he was listening to, so I went closer. At the touch of my hand on his shoulder, he jumped back and whirled around, wearing a guilty expression.

Before I could say anything, the two men and the woman from the ad agency came up from behind the trellis, passing through the arched walkway separating the patio from the beach. They were so involved in their conversation that they didn't even notice us standing there.

"Just trying to get some inside information." Jim laughed nervously.

Jim had been listening to the agency representatives!

"Did you hear anything interesting?" I asked.

He shook his head. "No, nothing worth spying for." Then he flashed his great smile, the same smile as on the poster. "Come on," he said. "You should lie down for a half hour before your big modeling debut. That's what I do."

"You're the expert," I said.

"That's right. I'll teach you everything I know."

I walked with him back toward the rooms as the sun burst out from behind the last rain cloud. What could be better?

Chapter Thirteen

Out on the beach, all eight models—five girls and three guys—stood together in a group. We'd been shooting pictures for about an hour. And we were having a blast!

"All right, Nikki," Pete, the photographer, said to me. "I think cartwheels would be fun here. Can you do them?"

"No problem," I replied cheerfully. I was modeling a pair of loose-fitting, yellow cotton pull-on pants and a hot-pink leotard, so it was easy to do a series of cartwheels along the shoreline. Pete got on his knees and moved along with me, shooting pictures as I went head over heels.

"Terrific," he said, which made me feel great. "Now I want some fun scenes in the water." He assigned Ashley and a cute, broad-shouldered, guy named Matt Ryan to get into the water and splash each other. Ashley shrieked with laughter as she and Matt had their water fight, but when she walked out of the ocean, her face grew serious.

"Anybody have sunblock?" she called. "Mine isn't waterproof."

"Here," said Rachel Wright, tossing a white tube toward Ashley. She wasn't a very good shot, and the tube landed on top of Jim's khaki canvas bag.

"Nice throw, Rachel," Ashley teased.

Playfully Rachel stuck out her tongue at Ashley as Jim went to his bag. He picked up the sunblock and then turned his back to us while he looked for something in his bag.

"Come on, Corcoran, I need that sunblock now," Ashley needled him. "Hand it over, *pronto*."

"Yes, your highness," said Jim, walking over to us with a smile.

"What is that stuff?" I asked as he handed her the plain, unmarked white tube.

"I don't know," said Jim, shrugging his shoulders.

"Oh, Rachel gets all her creams hand-blended at this super expensive place downtown," said Ashley. She slathered her arms with the thick white cream. "I've been meaning to try the place, but I never get down there."

When she was done, Jim asked Rachel if he could try her sunblock. "I think mine has washed off, too," he said.

"Okay, Jimmy, but don't use too much," Rachel agreed, tossing her short blond hair.

"Don't be so cheap," Jim taunted as he returned to his towel. He threw the tube into his bag and sat back down.

"Well, put it on already!" Rachel scolded him. "I need it back."

"It's not like I was going to steal it from you." He pulled it from his bag and began putting the cream on his arms. "Relax, would ya?"

We took pictures for two more hours. Pete often paired me with Pablo Ruiz, a tall guy with lots of gorgeous dark curls. By the end of the second hour, I was beat. "That's it for today," Pete announced. "See you tomorrow before it gets very hot. That's a six-thirty call."

"Six-thirty!" Tracey cried in dismay.

"I'm going straight to bed," said Ashley. "I've had it."

I looked at her and noticed she had a definite pinkish glow. "I think you got a little burned," I mentioned.

"It probably happened while I was in the water," she said, pressing her arm and watching a white fingerprint appear, the sure sign of a burn. "It takes a split second for me to burn." Her eyes suddenly went wide. "Hey, maybe that's what Renata meant about the threat from nature. Good thing she alerted me, otherwise I might have forgotten to put that sunblock on a second time."

All the models went back to their rooms looking pretty tired. When we got to our room, Tracey's mother was sitting on the balcony, sipping a tropical fruit drink out of a huge glass. Tracey immediately dialed room service and ordered shrimp cocktails, and then turned on the television.

It was heavenly stretching out on the big bed in front

of the television and eating ice-cold shrimp. While Tracey was in the middle of telling me how a counterfeiter might have made better fake money, the phone rang.

It was Chloe. "Thank goodness," she said when I answered. "Everyone's out doing something. Renata went to a restaurant over at some big hotel, but I don't remember which one and I don't know what to do. Is Tracey's mother there?"

"Yes, she is. What's wrong?"

"It's Ashley. She's covered with sunburn blisters. She's in terrible pain and we don't know what to do."

"We'll be right there," I said.

I told Tracey and her mom what was wrong, and we all rushed down the hall to the room Chloe and Ashley were sharing with Renata. "Oh, my dear!" Mrs. Morris gasped when she saw Ashley.

Ashley was bright red and her eyes were puffy. But worst of all, her arms and legs were covered with blisters the size of golf balls. Small, clear blisters also clustered along her nose and cheekbones.

"You can't believe how much this hurts," Ashley whimpered, sitting at the edge of her bed in a light nightshirt, rocking herself gently back and forth.

"Yes we can," Mrs. Morris said. "It looks very painful."

"But you put sunblock on," said Chloe.

"Rachel and Jim used it, too," Ashley said in a weak voice. "I wonder if they're okay."

"There's a number here for the resort infirmary," said

Tracey, looking through a list on the desk.

"We need a real doctor," Mrs. Morris said. "Tracey, have the front desk call us a cab."

Mrs. Morris found an extra white sheet in the closet. Gingerly she wrapped it around Ashley and walked her down to the front desk. Ashley cringed with every step she took. Her puffy eyes filled with tears and she bit her lip.

The cab was waiting when we got to the front door. Tracey's mother quickly left a message for Renata at the desk, and soon we were driving toward the hospital. Luckily the emergency room nurses took Ashley right away. Tracey's mother was the only one they would let go in with her.

"How could this have happened?" Chloe exploded in the waiting room. "She was so careful! She wasn't in the water that much. There had to have been something wrong with that cream. But I saw Jim and Rachel going to the soda machine not long ago. They were both fine."

"Maybe Ashley is allergic to the cream," Tracey suggested.

"She's not allergic to anything that I know about. Those blisters looked so horrible," Chloe said, taking a shaky breath. "I hope they don't leave scars. It's a good thing your mother was here, Tracey."

"Yeah, she's good in emergencies," Tracey agreed, looking around as if she was searching for something. "Anyone seen a soda machine? I get thirsty when I'm upset."

"There was one by the entrance," I told her.

When Tracey went off to the machine, Chloe and I sat silently. "This is so unfair!" Chloe said after a minute.

"I know," I agreed. "Ashley is so nice. She's made me feel like I have a friend at the agency and—" I stopped short, realizing Chloe wasn't the one to be saying this to.

"It's okay," said Chloe sadly. "That's how Ashley is." Suddenly she buried her face in her hands and cried.

I touched Chloe's shoulder. "She'll be all right," I said.

Just then Tracey returned from the soda machine and her mother came back out into the waiting room. "They want to keep her overnight," Mrs. Morris told us. "They've put antibiotic creams and bandages on, but they want to keep her in a sterile environment in case those blisters pop."

"Can I see her?" asked Chloe.

"Not tonight. They gave her some medicine and it's making her drowsy. You can see her in the morning."

All of us were quiet on the cab ride back to the hotel. Renata was waiting in the lobby. Chloe ran over to tell her what had happened.

Back in our room, Tracey, her mother, and I all got ready for bed. In a few minutes, Tracey's deep breathing and her mother's light snores told me they were asleep. Yet, tired as I was, I couldn't sleep.

Quietly I went out onto the balcony. A fat moon was reflected on the ocean, and the sound of the gently crashing surf was soothing. I suddenly felt a great desire to walk along the beach and think about everything that had happened.

I quickly pulled on some jeans and a T-shirt and slipped out of the dark hotel room, through the lobby, and outside. An island band played on the patio. Here and there people walked along, laughing and talking. But down on the beach, it was another world, quiet and dark.

With my hands shoved in my pockets, I walked by the shoreline, letting the water tickle my bare toes. I thought about Ashley and how her career would be over if the sunburn left bad scars. What would she do? Would she have to become a regular kid? I couldn't picture Ashley without her glamorous career.

Chloe was right. It was unfair. Ashley was still Ashley, scars or not. But then, modeling was about looking pretty. If Ashley didn't look pretty, she couldn't model.

I was all wrapped up in these thoughts as I turned a bend in the shoreline. I'd walked quite a way from the resort area, and the cove I'd turned into was especially dark. As I passed a boulder on the shore, something moved.

Startled, I jumped back and cried out. My heart pounded as I quickly backed up.

"Don't worry," a voice said out of the darkness. "It's just me, Jim."

Chapter Fourteen

Jim lit the fire he'd built from driftwood and stood back as it crackled to life. His face looked very handsome there in the darkness as the flames threw flickering lights across it. "There," he said. "At least now we can see each other."

"I guess you couldn't sleep, either," I said.

"No, I couldn't. There are a lot of things on my mind."

"Like what?" I asked, interested to know everything about him.

"Well, I was thinking about my singing career."

"You have a singing career, too?" I asked, impressed.

"Not yet. But I will. That's what I'd really like to be, a singer. I was trying to figure out a way to make it happen." As he spoke, he sat back in the sand and hugged his legs, letting his chin rest on his knees. "If I get to be the Cotton Kids spokesguy, that would be a big plus.

People would get to know me. That would be good for a singing career."

"Ms. Calico told me you're the favorite choice for the spot," I said encouragingly. "It's the girl they haven't decided on yet."

"That's changed," he said, frowning. "They've decided that the guy they pick depends on which girl they pick."

"I don't understand," I said.

"They've already narrowed it down to two girls, either Rachel or Ashley. They think I look good with Rachel, but I'm too tall to look good next to Ashley. They like Matt Ryan with Ashley because he's shorter."

"So, if they pick Rachel, you get the job, and if they pick Ashley, Matt gets the job?"

"Right."

"How do you know all this?" I asked.

Jim picked up a pebble and threw it into the fire. "That's what I heard today when I was listening to the ad agency representatives talking. I just happened to be walking by and I heard my name mentioned, so I stopped. That's when I heard the rest of it." Absently he threw a large stone into the fire. It tumbled the top piece of driftwood off the blaze, out of the stone circle he'd built around the fire.

"Oh!" I cried, jumping up as the flaming wood rolled toward us. In the glow of the fire, I saw that Jim's khaki canvas bag lay open on the sand beside him. "Watch out your bag doesn't catch fire!" I said.

Jim had jumped up, too. "It's okay," he said, kicking sand on the flaming wood.

We sat back down and Jim threw a few more pieces of wood on the fire. I was going to tell him about Ashley when something stopped me.

It was his bag.

There was a white tube lying inside it. I'd seen it in the glow of the fiery wood that had tumbled from the pile. It was the sunblock Ashley had put on that afternoon.

"You forgot to give Rachel back her sunblock," I observed.

Jim was busy stirring up the fire. "What?" he asked, more involved with the fire than with what I was saying.

"You have Rachel's sunblock," I repeated.

The fire started to die, and Jim tried to fan it back to life with his hand. "Oh, no, that's my hand cream. Rachel and I go to the same place to have those creams made. They come in the same unmarked tubes." The fire died down even further. "Darn! I must have put damp wood on here."

While he was busy with the fire, my mind was racing. Something didn't add up. He'd told Ashley he didn't know what kind of cream Rachel had. This afternoon he'd acted as if he'd never seen it before.

I was suddenly struck with a horrifying realization. "You gave Ashley the wrong cream!" I blurted out.

Jim looked up sharply from the fire. The expression on his face told me everything. I've never seen anyone look more guilty. It hadn't been an accident!

"You did it on purpose. The tube fell near your things and you switched them. Then you took the hand cream back to your towel and switched it with the sunblock!"

Jim stared at me like a cornered animal. "That's crazy," he said. "Why would I do something like that?"

"You just told me why!" I shouted. "I'm not stupid. If they picked Ashley, then Matt Ryan would get the job, not you!"

Again his shamed, guilty face gave him away. I knew I'd gotten it right. "That's so hateful and horrible!" I cried. "You put Ashley in the hospital. How could you do that?"

"What?" he said in alarm. "What are you talking about?"

"She's covered with blisters!"

"I didn't... I... Are you sure?"

"I saw her myself."

Jim shook his head. "No, that wasn't supposed to happen. It couldn't have."

"Well, it did," I said angrily. "Does it mean that much to you to represent Cotton Kids?"

"I need this job," he said, giving up his pretense of innocence. "I'm sixteen and I want to move into my singing career. Matt Ryan is just a goof-off. He couldn't care less about his career. He's not serious, but I am. I'm better-looking, and I act much more professional. I'm ready for this job! I'm so prepared, I even called ahead to tell them how to make my health shake for tomorrow morning. I deserve the job, not him."

"What about Ashley?" I challenged him angrily.

"I didn't think she'd land in the hospital. Honestly. How could I have known she would burn so easily? I only wanted her to get too red for the shoot."

"You didn't care what you did as long as you got the job," I said. "That's the real truth."

I couldn't stand to look at him anymore. His face no longer seemed handsome. He looked devilish. I turned and began walking off.

"Nikki, wait!" Jim called after me.

I stopped and looked back at him. "You won't tell anyone, will you?" he asked, making his big blue eyes look all soft and puppylike. "It's not like I planned to do this or anything. The tube practically fell in my lap, and it gave me the idea. I did it on impulse. I didn't mean to hurt Ashley."

I turned my back on him and hurried along the shore.

"No one will believe you!" he shouted after me. "You have no proof!"

When I got back to the resort, there were still a few people moving around. I crossed the lawn between the hotel and the beach and looked up to my second-story room. I saw Tracey standing on the balcony in her nightshirt. She saw me at the same time and waved.

Why was she up? Had Ashley gotten worse? I broke into a run across the lawn. Tracey met me when I was halfway up the outside stairs. "Where were you?" she asked.

"Taking a walk. Why are you up? Is Ashley all right?"

"We haven't heard any more about her," she assured

me. "I woke up and saw you were gone. I got worried." She stepped back and studied my face. "Hey, are you okay? You look really upset."

I sat on the top step of the landing. "Listen to what I just found out." I told her the whole story.

"That rat!" she fumed.

"You should have heard him making up excuses about why he deserves the job more than anyone else." I puffed up my chest and imitated Jim. "'I'm better-looking. I'm more professional. I even called ahead to tell them how to make my health shake.'"

"He called about his health drink!" Tracey cried in disbelief. "Talk about taking yourself too seriously."

"Do you think we should tell Renata?" I asked her.

She scrunched her mouth in thought. "We could," she answered after a moment. "But Jim is right. There's no real proof, just circumstantial evidence, as they say on TV."

"But he admitted it to me," I reminded her.

"Yeah, but he'll deny it if you turn him in."

"Then what should we do?" I asked.

"There must be some way to get him back for this," she mused.

"Like what?"

"I don't know yet, but believe me, I'm putting every ounce of brainpower to work on this problem right now."

Chapter Fifteen

When I opened my eyes the next morning, both Tracey and her mother were out of bed. The hazy light told me it was dawn. Why were they up? Then I remembered that I was supposed to be on the beach by six-thirty.

"Good morning," said Mrs. Morris, coming inside from the balcony. "I was just going to wake you. Tracey's already down by the patio eating breakfast. She bolted out of bed at five o'clock. I've never seen her so energetic in the morning."

What could she be up to? I quickly dressed in shorts and a T-shirt. Still half-asleep, I stumbled to the patio. When I got there, the waiters were setting up the tables for breakfast. Tracey was the only customer. She sat alone eating a huge breakfast of eggs, toast, and home fries. "You're up bright and early," I commented as I slumped into a seat beside her.

When the waiter came, I ordered some juice and a bowl

of cereal. A few other guests began seating themselves for breakfast. I glared at Jim as he took a table. He glanced at me quickly and then turned away. In a few minutes, he was joined by Rachel, Matt Ryan, and Pablo Ruiz.

A bit later, Chloe came down from her room, dressed in jeans and a neon pink cropped top. She waved and joined us at our table. She seemed to have forgotten her dislike for me. Something had changed between us last night while we were at the hospital. It was as if we were now united by our common concern for Ashley.

"I called the hospital this morning," Chloe told us. "They said Ashley is okay. They want her in bed for a while longer, though, so she won't be discharged till Sunday morning."

"I'm glad she's okay," I said. Then I told her what I'd learned last night about Jim and the sunblock.

Chloe's dark eyes grew even darker with anger. "I'm telling Renata right now."

"Tracey and I aren't sure anyone will believe us," I said. I looked over at Tracey, expecting her to add something, but from her expression I could tell she was a million miles away. I followed her gaze and saw that she was staring at Jim as he gave his breakfast order to the waiter.

"I wish I could read lips," she muttered.

"Why?" I asked.

"Then I would know what he ordered for breakfast."

"Why do you care?" asked Chloe.

"Chloe wants to tell Renata about Jim," I told Tracey,

"but I was saying we weren't sure if—"

"No, no," Tracey said, holding up her hand. "Not yet. Let's see if my plan works first."

"You came up with a plan!" I gasped.

"Shhh!" Tracey hissed sharply. "A brilliant plan, but it might not work." Once again her attention shifted away from us. Her steady gaze followed the path of a waiter who was bringing a shiny silver shaker to Jim's table. "Yes!" Tracey cheered under her breath. "He's having the shake."

"Tell me what is going on!" I demanded, unable to bear it anymore.

"Be patient. You'll find out," she promised.

When breakfast was almost over, Renata came to our table. She looked very pale and had deep circles under her eyes. I guessed that she'd been up all night worrying about Ashley. "Here's the schedule, kids," she said. "We'll bus you all over to Horseshoe Bay Beach and do another group shoot. Then we'll break for lunch. During lunch we'll announce who the spokeskids will be—probably Jim and Rachel, but the agency reps haven't officially made their final choice. Then everyone else will do some catalog shots, while the new spokeskids go into the town of Hamilton to do some special photos. There might even be a short spot on the local TV station for the spokeskids. We're still getting that together. We'll do more shots on Sunday morning, and we have a noon flight out of here."

"That's a lot for one weekend," I commented.

"It sure is," said Renata. "But it's always like this."

Soon we went up to the main lobby, where the minivans were waiting. Then we drove along the winding roads to Horseshoe Bay Beach. The moment we arrived, I knew why Pete had wanted to shoot there. The sand is actually pink, and big, arching coral formations jut out into the aqua blue ocean.

We'd only been there ten minutes when Tracey nudged my arm. "Look at Jim Corcoran," she said with a smile.

I looked over to where he stood with his feet in the surf, and noticed that he was absently scratching his face. "It's starting," Tracey said.

Just then Chloe joined us. "What are the two of you staring at?"

"A rash," Tracey said.

"What?" Chloe asked.

"I arranged to have two strawberries put in Jim's health drink this morning."

"How did you do that?" I whispered.

Tracey smiled broadly. "I called the patio dining room. I said I was Jim's agent and I was checking to make sure they knew how to make his health shake correctly. They read me the ingredients, and I started making this big fuss about how they forgot the two strawberries." She began speaking in a high-pitched, fussy voice: "Oh, the strawberries are most important. We must, *must* have the strawberries!"

"And they did it!" Chloe said, gazing at Jim as if she couldn't believe her eyes. "Look at him now."

We watched Jim as he bent down and began scratching

his legs. He held up his arms, and a look of horror spread across his face as he realized that a rash was showing up all over him.

"I don't know if you should have done that," I said, worried. "It might be dangerous."

"I wouldn't have done it if it was dangerous," Tracey insisted. "Don't you remember? He said it wasn't a big deal—just that it didn't look too attractive in pictures."

Chloe chewed on her thumbnail anxiously. "I don't know," she mumbled. "Maybe you shouldn't have."

"Ah, come on, I didn't hurt him," said Tracey. "I only gave him a taste of his own medicine."

I looked at Jim again and saw that he wasn't in real pain. He was just itchy as anything. "I guess you're right," I said. "He deserves a little itching after what he did to Ashley."

As the shoot went on, Jim itched more and more. "Are you getting sunburned, Jim?" Pete asked him. "You're getting sort of red."

"No, it's this stupid rash!" Jim said, scratching angrily. "I don't know what could be causing it."

I felt a strange mixture of guilt and satisfaction as I watched Jim scratch. Once I saw that he was fine except for the rash, the guilt faded. I had to admit I was glad that he'd been paid back for what he'd done.

With Jim scratching all the way, we drove back to the hotel in the minivans. Soon we would find out who would be named the Cotton Kids spokeskids. Now that Jim and Ashley couldn't win the job, I wondered who would be picked. It would be wild if it was me, but I knew I'd never be so lucky on my first modeling job.

Well, I guess I don't know everything, because at lunch the most unbelievable thing happened. "Our two Cotton Kids spokeskids are Pablo Ruiz and Nikki Wilton!" Renata announced. Everyone clapped. Tracey and Chloe stood up and cheered. I smiled until my face hurt.

Of course I knew I'd been selected only because Ashley and Jim were out of the running—which put their partners, Matt and Rachel, out of the running, too. Still, I *had* won and it was a great opportunity.

I spent the rest of that afternoon shooting pictures with Pablo all around Hamilton, the capital of Bermuda. It's an elegant, hilly place, full of colorful shops. We stood in front of monuments, sea walls, and at the Bermuda Zoo, always wearing our Cotton Kids clothing. I got to know Pablo better, too.

On Sunday morning I was actually in a TV commercial. All we did was appear in Cotton Kids jogging suits and yell, "Cotton Kids love Bermuda!" But it was pretty exciting.

The time zoomed by so fast that by noon on Sunday, I could hardly believe I was standing in the Bermuda airport waiting to go home. "There she is," Chloe cried when Renata came into the airport waiting room with Ashley.

"How are you feeling?" I asked as Chloe, Tracey, and I surrounded her.

"Like a human torch," Ashley said, smiling weakly. "But they gave me lots of creams to keep away infection, and they say if I rest and use the medicines, everything should be fine. There probably won't even be any scars."

"All right!" I said.

On the plane ride, we sat together in two sets of seats across the aisle from each other. We told Ashley what Tracey had done to Jim. "That was nice of you to do for me," she said to Tracey. "Well, maybe it wasn't exactly nice, but I appreciate it. I knew you were a cool person from the minute I met you. I'm a very good judge of people."

Tracey and Ashley napped during the flight home, but Chloe and I stayed awake. "I'm sorry I was so mean to you when we first met," Chloe said in a quiet voice. "You didn't deserve it."

"It's all right," I said. "No one wants to lose a friend. But it isn't going to be that way. I think you and Ashley will always be best friends. I hope we can be friends, too."

Chloe smiled warmly. "We can," she said.

Out of curiosity, I looked over to where Jim Corcoran was sitting. His rash had faded and he was fine, although he looked miserable. I thought it was sad that being successful was so important to him that he would hurt someone to get ahead. I swore to myself that I would never become like that.

I slid down in my seat and thought about Dee and Kathy. Had they enjoyed the dance? Would they be interested in hearing about my trip? Or were we now living in worlds so different that we would never really understand each other again?

Suddenly I felt very anxious about going home.

Chapter Sixteen

———•———

Is anyone looking?" Ashley asked, peeking over her shoulder down the green-carpeted hall of the Calico Modeling Agency.

"All clear," I reported.

Quickly she opened the door to the Red Room and slipped in. Chloe went in behind her and then I followed, pulling Tracey with me.

Ashley flipped on the red light. "Here it is," she said to Tracey. "The Red Room. Your place to go when you need a break, need a nap, or need to think."

Tracey took off her glasses and looked around. "This is so creepy and cool," she said with approval. "Hey, Ashley, this is the one room where you don't look too red."

"Don't remind me," said Ashley. The agency had sent a limo to pick us up at the airport and drop us off here. Tracey and I had some time to kill before Eve picked us up, so Ashley suggested we spend it in the Red Room.

Ashley cleared her throat. "I have an announcement," she said. "For quick thinking and guts, we honor you, Tracey Morris, and make you an official Red Room member."

"Thanks," said Tracey. "I'll keep your secret to the death."

Then Ashley turned to me. "You're an official member, too, Nikki—just for being generally cool. Chloe says it's fine with her."

Chloe smiled at me. I was glad that old hurt look was gone from her eyes. She really *was* ready to be friends.

I looked at Ashley, Tracey, and Chloe, and I couldn't believe how close I'd grown to them in such a short time. All my life my only close friends had been Kathy and Dee. It was exciting to be making new friends.

Yet as Eve drove us home that afternoon, I couldn't stop thinking about Kathy and Dee. Was I willing to let them fade out of my life?

After we dropped off Tracey and her mom, Eve and I went home. When we pulled in the driveway, I saw a big banner reading WELCOME HOME, NIKKI! strung across the garage door. From the scraggly writing, I guessed that Todd had made it.

My mom, Martin, and Todd all came running out of the house to greet me as if I'd been gone for months. It might have been a little silly, but it felt good.

I dragged my suitcase upstairs and immediately took

Jim's poster off the wall. Then I began unpacking. Carefully I took out four seashell necklaces I'd bought in Hamilton. One was for my mother. Another was for Eve.

Just then Eve came in, gabbing with someone on the cordless phone. "See you tomorrow. Bye," she said as she clicked off and tossed the phone on the bed.

"I brought one of these home for you," I said, offering her the pink necklace.

"You did?" she said, gingerly picking it up from my outstretched palm. "It's pretty. Is it shells?"

"Yeah. It's to say thanks for driving me into the city and stuff, and that, you know, I was thinking of you."

Eve frowned skeptically. "You were?"

"Once in a while," I said with a small laugh. "Strange but true."

That made Eve smile. "I thought about you once in a while, too. Thanks for the necklace."

"You're welcome."

Eve left the room, still turning the necklace over in her hands as if she couldn't believe I'd actually given it to her. I was glad I had.

I looked at the two other necklaces, and I picked up the phone. Quickly I punched in Dee's familiar number. "Hi, it's me," I said when she answered.

"How was it?" she asked, sounding a little cautious. It was like she wasn't sure how to talk to me anymore.

I told her all about Bermuda and asked about the dance. "It was great, Nikki, but I'll have to tell you about it later. Kathy is waiting for me downstairs. We're going to the movies." There was a pause. Then Dee added, almost shyly, "I guess you're probably too pooped from your flight to come with us."

"No, I'm not," I said. "I can come right over. I want to hear all about the dance, and I have a little present for each of you."

"Well, come on," Dee said happily. "We'll wait at my house."

I scooped up the necklaces and grabbed my denim jacket as I dashed out of the room. It was strange to think that this morning I'd awakened on a tropical island, been in a television commercial, and then jetted home. Now I was running out to the mall to meet my friends, just like any normal kid.

I remembered Martin saying that it would take work to keep my old friends as I moved into a new world. But I was so happy at the thought of seeing Kathy and Dee that I knew I wanted to keep their friendship.

I'd learned something in Bermuda. It was important to have friends. New ones and old ones.

And if making time for Dee and Kathy meant some extra effort on my part, well — I was ready to work at it.